*The Wrong Music*

# THE WRONG MUSIC
## The Poems of Olive Fraser
### 1909–1977

*Edited by Helena M. Shire*

CANONGATE

First published in 1989
by Canongate Publishing Limited,
17 Jeffrey Street, Edinburgh.

© 1989 Helena M. Shire

The publisher acknowledges subsidy of
the Scottish Arts Council towards the
publication of this volume.

*British Library Cataloguing in Publication Data*
Fraser, Olive, *1909–1977*
The wrong music: the poems of Olive Fraser
1909–1977
I. Title   II. Shire, Helena M. (Helena Mennie)
821′.914
ISBN 0 86241 217 X

Typeset by Speedspools, Edinburgh.
Printed and bound in Great Britain by
Billings & Sons Limited, Worcester.

# Contents

*The 'Wonderful Years', Aberdeen: Hospital and Holidays, 1970–1973*

## ACKNOWLEDGEMENTS

My most sincere thanks to all of Olive Fraser's friends who have
helped me to assemble her poems and recover her life-story. They
will find how much I owe them in happy context in this book. My
particular thanks to my sister and brother who provided matter and
counsel on what has been a Mennie-family project. To Mr and Mrs
Charles Jeans and their daughter Norma I am deeply grateful for
returning the author's amassed papers to Europe for me to study and
for encouraging me to publish. The copyright of Olive Fraser's
work, at first mistakenly allotted to them, fell legally to much nearer

kin, first cousins of Olive's on her father's side; these most generously granted it to me, and I thank them warmly for this.

Special thanks to Kathleen Raine, who at a critical juncture asserted her faith in Olive Fraser's poetry as of real distinction. On the practical side a great debt to the patience and insight of Christine Pollitt and Ian Peacocke who indexed a mass of inchoate papers. And my warm thanks to Canongate and Joy Hendry for their skills and interest at the production stage and to two kind Celtic scholars, Professor Gillies and Ian MacDonald who gave advice on Gaelic matters.

Above all my gratitude in remembrance to C. J. Hamson, Q.C., for his championing of Olive's poetry and his voiced companionship through seven years of search and study.

In 1981 A.U.P. had the imagination to print some 30 of Olive Fraser's poems, from the texts then available, in *The Pure Account*. By their courtesy we here reprint the poems acknowledged below.

Helena Mennie Shire

The poems listed below have appeared in previous publications. The dates in italics denote the earliest record of the poem, ms or print; the dates in parentheses give dates of publication.

*1930:* 'Christopher steals' *Alma Mater* (Aberdeen University Magazine), Vol.XLVII, p.186, 20 February (1930); *The Pure Account*, Aberdeen University Press (A.U.P.) (1981).

*1930:* 'Grey Goose Walking' *Alma Mater*, Vol.XLVIII, p.248, 30 April (1931).

*1935:* 'The Vikings' *Prolusiones Academicae*, Cambridge University Press (C.U.P.) (1935); *The Girton Review*, Summer 1935, Cambridge (1935); *Contemporaries*, Vol.2, No.1, Cambridge, Summer (1935); *The Pure Account*, A.U.P. (1981).

*1936:* 'Envoi to Poetry' *The Pure Account* (variants in text), A.U.P. (1981).

*1941:* 'The Sleeper' *Temenos*, Vol.9 (annual anthology) (1988).

*1945?:* 'V.E. Day 1945' *New Scots Poetry*, Serif Books, Edinburgh (1952); reprinted *Lines Review*, No.82, M. Macdonald, Edinburgh (1982).

*1946:* 'Upon an Irish Terrier, Quip' (Epitaphs 1 and 2) *The Pure Account*, A.U.P. (1981).

*1946:* 'The King's Student' *Aberdeen University Review*, Summer (1946); reprinted *Aberdeen University Review*, Autumn (1983); *The Pure Account* (variants in text), A.U.P. (1981).

*1947:* 'The Mountain Bird/The Dipper' *The Nairnshire Telegraph* (date unknown) (c.1947); also in 'The River Gang, Reminiscences' by O.F., *The Mercat Cross*, Vol.12, No.2, February (1957).

*1949:* 'The Tree' in 'A Poet Rediscovered' by H. M. Shire, *The Tablet*, I, September (1984).

# Introduction

The publication of this volume affords an unusual delight, the discovery of a new voice in Scottish, indeed in British poetry. Here the best of a life's work in poetic creation is offered all at once, by far the greater part of it printed for the first time— surely an unusual circumstance. It is twelve years since Olive Fraser died. She would have been eighty years old this January. How did it come about that a hoard of outstanding poetry remained unknown? She was early a prizewinner in poetic contest at Aberdeen University and at Cambridge for English verse, and for Scots verse she won a high award in the national contest in 1951 (Festival of Britain Year) for lyric and for verse drama. But ill health, insidious from her student days on, then shattering experience under wartime fire culminated in mental illness and many years under hospital care. With this went persistent crippling poverty. It is small wonder that her poetry, which she continued to write under miserable or agonising conditions, reached publication very seldom, now here now there, and on occasions many years apart.

Who was she? What her ancestry was she herself never knew for certain. The only thing she was sure of was her Christian name Olive. And in these five letters, in order, in reverse or in anagram, she perceived a definition of her identity, its inner conflict, for they spell O LIVE, I LOVE but also EVIL O and O VILE. Committed to this name she grew up with a deep schism in her personality— love and hate, a discord of life matched only by the concord of her poetry. She expressed it also in astrological terms: that her stars were two: Betelgeuse bringer of all talents and honours and Algol, the most malevolent star in the heavens, the eye of the dragon in Perseus, bringer of mischief and evil chance. Under their influence her strange life was lived.

I

*The Unwanted Child*

I was the wrong music
The wrong guest for you
When I came thro' the tundras
And thro' the dew.

Summon'd, tho unwanted,
Hated, tho' true
I came by golden mountains
To dwell with you.

I took strange Algol with me
And Betelgueuse, but you
Wanted a purse of dust
And interest to accrue.

You could have had them all,
The dust, the glories too,
But I was the wrong music
And why I never knew.

26 January, 1971

Olive Fraser belonged to Nairn. She was the only child of Roderick Fraser, a farmer's son from Flemington on the road to Inverness and Elizabeth King, also of country stock, whose grandfather John Jeans had farmed at Balmakeith near Nairn. Olive's parents had married secretly 'before the Sheriff' in Old Aberdeen in 1908. Very soon afterwards Roderick Fraser emigrated to Australia.

Olive was born at the home of a great-aunt in Torry, that part of Aberdeen that lies south of the River Dee in Kincardine. The year was 1909, the day January the twentieth, 'St Agnes' Eve', a date she treasured as 'my romantic birthright, the one thing I would not change with anyone.' A year or so later Mrs Fraser followed her husband out to Australia, to Melbourne. Olive grew up in Nairn in the loving care of her great-aunt, Miss Ann Maria Jeans, in 'Redburn', the beautiful old house in Queen Street that had been the home of Jeans womenfolk since early in the century. Miss Jeans took paying guests who were teachers at Nairn Academy.

At Nairn she went to school, to Millbank then to Rose's Academical Institution. Nairn was a wonderful place to grow up in. 'The cobbled port' she called it, a small old seaport on the sheltered coast of the Moray Firth, with its own river-mouth and little river flowing past the end of the High Street. There town ended and beautiful countryside began—rich farmland, woods, a castle or two and hills within sight. A street or two away from her home there were the river meadows to play in, with a ruined church and a deserted orchard. The river and its birds and happiness of childhood adventuring sound through her poetry to the end.

Olive ran happily wild under Miss Jeans' loving eye. In her schooldays the young natives of Nairn fought the summer bucket-and-spaders and also fought the young of the fisher-folk, who though indigenous were strictly apart in kin and traditions, the fishers being the 'first chosen', as is said in the northeast. These years she described, no doubt with a spice of fiction, in 'The River Gang; Reminiscences of a Highland Childhood': 'I was running about climbing trees and pushing (schoolboy) classical scholars into rivers at an age when girls in the south would be painting their faces and having boy–friends. We—the Hendries, the Bowies, the Cruickshanks, the Mackintoshes—were dangling from the parapets of bridges, flying from pursuing gamekeepers, having glorious hair-breadth escapes . . .'

This untrammeled youth was sharply reined in when her mother returned from Australia after the war and attempted to discipline her daughter. Olive was nine years old. Both the discipline and the earlier absence were deeply resented and a build-up of hostility began between mother and daughter. A set of schoolgirl verses records this and through these we glimpse the mother already afflicted by the arthritis that was soon to disable her entirely.

Her father had returned from Australia during the war because by 1917 he could no longer earn his living. He too was disabled by severe arthritis. He had to return to the farm at Flemington where he was cared for by his mother and sister. How badly he had behaved to his wife in Australia we may never know but after the war the two lived estranged, each in the family home; these lay only a few miles apart but there was little contact. Among the Frasers the child

3

Olive was never mentioned nor was Roderick's marriage. What is never mentioned does not exist.

The impact on an imaginative child of this strange pattern of parenthood must have been sharp and deep. To have a father away in Australia and subject of who-knows-what fantasising—and then to have him back in Scotland but inaccessible, suddenly present to the adolescent schoolgirl as a source of gifts but still not a 'real' father who could be claimed as such! At one point Olive remarked to a friend: 'The family gave me presents, books, lovely clothes, a gold watch—but no affection.' She meant 'the Frasers' but she did not use the name.

This silence so faithfully observed had one bizarre effect. During her College years in Aberdeen Olive had three first-cousins on her father's side of roughly her own age living at home in the same city as she, but entirely ignorant of her existence. Nor had they heard that their invalid Uncle Roddie had ever been married, or had a child—so well can highlanders keep close lips and promises made.


*At College: Aberdeen and Cambridge*

The years of wild play had been at the same time years of serious and distinguished work in school (except for mathematics where she was a dunce). From these in 1927 she came to Aberdeen University to King's College to do Honours English. There she made her mark at once. She was notably good-looking—rosy cheeked, yellow haired and with a penetrating blue gaze. She was full of life and fun—and she could talk. In a College Society debate I recall a peroration on Desdemona—'She was the pure and perfect chrysolite, she was the lantern at the mast—and she was innocent.' And the muttered comment from the male opposition, 'She niver thocht that up hersel', 'Faur did she get it fae?'

'She was a beauty—but she gave the men a run for it' and 'Not Florimel—more Atalanta.' (These comments come from fellow-students after more than half a century has passed.) She did brilliantly well in all her studies, not only English and History but also Zoology, 'Moral Phil.' and 'Greek Art and Thought'. In her first year she won the Calder Prize for English verse, a triennial award in the university, coveted among the young lyric-writers then at

4

college. King's College—with English Studies led by Professor Adolphus Alfred Jack, lovingly termed 'The Old Bird'—was known to nourish poetry writers, 'his nest of singing birds.'

In her fourth year she shared the same prize. Her poem was called 'Fugue of Morning'. Some twenty masterly Spenserean stanzas long, it had as epigraph *quo fugit venator per silvam per vitam?* We her friends had been listening to passages from it as it got written. Chanted aloud it was compelling.

> I. The snow of all the Appenine is gone
>     Down to the chasms of the summer. Lie
> The old range of the Alps like to a stone
>     Which nature framed of the light porphyry.
> Now wakes the hare. Now the mergansers fly
>     Like ghosts around the mountain tops. The swan
> And the wild dotteril of the hills all lie
>     Scattered in their dark sleeping-holes upon
> The lonely cliffs until silence and sleep are done . . .

> XX. So hunter, run the merry horn along
>     The haunted floors of forests, hear thy horse
> Most fiercely beat the ancient running song
>     Which Charlemain evoked from the old course
> Of the Pyrenez when his darling force,
>     His cavalcades over the rocks of Spain
> Poured their black warsong and the horn's remorse
>     Of the great Roland struck that lonely plain.
> Roland and thou shall ride to Roncevalles again.

Some of it we found beyond us. We perceived great themes of love and death and poetry but did not follow the concept of 'hunt is pursuit and flight' and we picked up only a few of the resonances sounded. She only laughed and said 'Listen. And read.'

Her years at King's College in Old Aberdeen, then, were of happy endeavour and achievement. 'It was the nearest thing you could get to a Platonic academia,' she said in old age looking back. In fact it was the depths of the economic depression when students were really poor.

We became firm friends and she called often at my home, only a short walk from King's, where students were welcomed warmly by my mother at any hour and fed scones and tea. There they could count on being wished luck for their essay or for their exams—ritually, with a shoe thrown after them to the door as they left. Olive recalled my mother's reputation for 'a lucky hand', remembering in her old age the lucky stone-with-a-hole-in-it my mother had given her before her Finals. 'She liked to talk also with my father, but he had reservations about prolonging discussion, however absorbing, into the small hours. One evening about eleven she whistled up to my window, student fashion. Down at the door I found her in some distress—an exam tomorrow and her watch had failed her. In my father's study she began her tale. But he could rise to Olive's occasion . . . "Tak the clock, lassie!" he said, reaching it down for her from the mantelpiece, folding it into her arms and guiding her down to the door, *"tempus fugit."* "Aye, puir lassie!" he said one day. I could not see why, but one did not ask my father questions.' [This anecdote is in *The Pure Account,* p.x.]

During our student days Olive spoke of her great-aunt often, and always with the greatest admiration, gratitude and affection. Her mother she never mentioned. Her father came sometimes into the conversation, in a throw-away phrase: 'My father sent me a fiver', 'I've had a telegram'. We gathered that he was somewhere, elsewhere, and had been sheep-farming in Australia, but we were not curious. Our interests centred on our own generation and on the future. The quasi–sonnet of 1930, 'To a Parent' was certainly not shown about at that time.

Friendship with Olive meant living a life keyed half-a-tone above normal. Emergencies sprouted in her path. I recall one family lunchtime being astonished to receive a telegram: 'Imprisoned in digs. Please rescue. Olive.' I ran to her lodgings a few streets away, and found her imprisoned indeed. She had dismantled a new fishing-rod there, the line had entangled her and she had then panicked, ending up bound like a spider's fly so that she could not open the door. But she called from the window to a passing boy, threw him a shilling for the telegram and a shilling to send it . . .

Olive was lucky in her year, an outstanding one in Honours English where the women students became a band of friends, arguing and making merry and on occasion spending a holiday together, once in the mountains at Tomintoul in a cottage owned by the mother of one of them. They were Isabel Sharp, Helen Stevens, Margaret Sutherland, Lesley Chalmers, Davidina Bonner and Jean B.W. Sinclair. In this group Olive found her peers in quick intelligence and witty talk. She could be the life and soul of the party, but sometimes the fun could go to her head and then she would overstep the bounds, grab the limelight and exasperate her fellows.

On one holiday occasion the girls had gathered berries and some had spent a hot and hectic hour making jam. A visitor arrived and Olive seized a crimson jar and carried it aloft in triumph. 'Look, we've been making jelly!' 'And not a handsturn had *she* done' came in a wrathful undertone. But Olive was caught up in the hot crisis of cookery, if not in the scene of action, and overcome with delight to be part of it all. Something of all this is caught in lines Olive wrote for fun, 'Apple land and fallow gray', to mark the holiday at New Pitsligo, the last they would spend together.

After a brilliant final year at King's College, Aberdeen, Olive was to go on to Cambridge with a Scottish University scholarship for further study. But she did not go, and why will never be clear. Perhaps she was unwell, exhausted. Perhaps it was a matter of expense. Her mother had been crippled by arthritis for some years. Her greataunt had helped her through her studies keeping 'Redburn' full of paying guests. But she was aged now and infirm. Apparently for this further study no financial help was forthcoming from her father or his family, though they may well have lent a helping hand up to this point. Certainly for two years Olive stayed in the north, mostly in Nairn, 'writing, tutoring, helping on a friend's farm. It was a fruitful time for poetry.' A letter she wrote to me in the summer of 1933, although light-hearted, shows the forecast as not without shadows.

The Lightning Dry Cleaners,
99 London Street,
Reading . . .

My dear Helena,
This scribble (written between dyeing the purple hat pink and the grey dress apple green) means that I am having a marvellous time . . . I wonder if you are in Yorkshire now. I hope you are having as good a time as I am.

By the way, Miss Hoare came to see me in Nairn when I was not well enough to go to see her . . . I am so glad she is at Cambridge. I have had a most thrilling experience the details of which I shall tell you sometime. My head became very bad with the South of England climate and I nearly threw up the idea of going to Cambridge. Then my employers took me to one of the great Harley Street specialists, who is dead nuts on psycho-analysis. In five days he made me more fit than months of the other treatment had done. You have no idea of the difference he made. He simply took my mind to pieces and bult it up again. I really feel as if I had been presented with a new heaven and a new earth, ten thousand cold showers on spring mornings and a Tinglow friction brush (mental)

Write to me sometime . . .

Yours ever,
Olive Fraser

In 1933 Olive came up to Girton College while I, having overtaken her in years of study, went to Newnham. She was twenty-four years past and found the discipline of undergraduate study—the weekly supervision essay, the sanctions of life in a women's college—untenable. We enjoyed together listening to lectures where I. A. Richards read Auden and Yeats to us or explored Coleridge on the imagination and Mansfield Forbes fantasticated on peel-towers as erotic symbols or chanted Blake's 'Voice of the Bard' or the 'Poison Tree'. But she complained of the dull heavy air, the dank inland smell, of bad headaches and great lassitude.

In a seminar that included some formidable personalities—Glyn Daniel, John Danby, Grace Thornton—she bemused Professor Chadwick with her fantastic conjectures on the clash or combination of Celtic and Nordic elements in northern Scotland, names of far-off places rippling from her tongue. In poetry-reading sessions at 'The Merry Meeting' in St. John's Street she recited her lyrics and gained a name as a young poet. She would appear in Cambridge with a trail of laughing companions, largely men and women in their first year.

Girton was finding her a troublesome charge. 'She wasted the time of promising young scholars' (as her tutor said) in sessions of hilarious conviviality or of sad lamentation of her troubles. In the words of a contemporary, Professor Muriel Bradbrook, when told

8

in 1980 that Olive's poems had been recovered: 'She was a pain in the neck.'

But already she was seriously ill. Her face had a grey tinge—at any rate to my eye, who had known her younger and flourishing in the north. The doctors could not agree as to what was wrong. Anaemia was suggested and for a term she endured a diet of raw liver. Her powers of study seriously flagged. She had terrible headaches with violent nose-bleeding. When it came to the examinations she was withdrawn from the Tripos on medical advice. Now her status both in College and university was precarious. (Girton has, I understand, a huge file on the complications of her health and studies.) She was granted the grace of a third year and support for it from Scottish funds, but with no better outcome. Eventually, with Girton's help, she was 'allowed a B.A.'.

But she brought honour to the College when in spring 1935 she won the Chancellor's Medal for English Verse, the first woman to do so. The subject of the poem was 'The Vikings'.

The recitation of the poem in the Senate House was a momentous occasion. A kind of quasi-academic dress had to be devised—and most effective it was—as women were still non-members of the university and had no right to gown and square. After this success Olive began to spell her name Olave, which she reckoned could render Celtic-bardic overtones with a suggestion of a feminine form of Olaf, expressing the Nord and Celt in her.

One memory of Olive in her third year at Cambridge disquiets me to this day. She was standing in Market Hill, in the doorway of Joshua Taylor's, looking across the traffic. She was wearing her old but valid Harris-tweed suit and had a long shepherd's crook in her hand. She had dressed her hair so that by each cheek hung a short thick plait—after the fashion of a Viking warrior. But on her feet she had silver dancing-sandals.

In the summer of 1936 she brought Oliver Zangwill to call on us—I had recently married. They had just returned from a hilarious spell of holiday canoeing on the River Wye. In his old age Oliver was happy to recall 'That summer I was writing my fellowship thesis (on experimental psychology). I simply gave what companionship I could. As a person she was life-enhancing.' With kind concern for her later ill-fortune he kept in some touch with her till the end of her days. In the last years of her life Olive reported she was 'rereading

9

an instruction-book we wrote on how to shoot rapids on the Wye and laughing immoderately over it.'

Her going-down from Cambridge that summer of 1936 was in some triumph as a poet but in wretched health and with poor prospects as a human being. Jobs were hard to get, especially for anyone with a chequered record. It would seem that at this point of low fortunes and insidiously encroaching illness someone took occasion to tell Olive of certain vicious and distressful passages in the past between her father and her mother in Australia. Small wonder that despair welled up in those dark verses of farewell to the muse

> Then get thee to Prosperpina, my light
> And leave me to my everlasting night.
>
> ('Envoi to Poetry')

This is where my personal knowledge of Olive Fraser ends. Her Cambridge friends lost sight of her, as did fellow students of Aberdeen days. From time to time someone heard something: she was learning to train polo-ponies in Oxfordshire or working for a recluse archeologist in Berkshire. A newspaper article she wrote years later, on strange employments, may reflect something of her fortunes after Cambridge. One document that gives a version of her history over the next twelve years, is a *curriculum vitae* she prepared when applying for a job in the Bodleian Library after the war. For the years 1936 to 1939 it reads: 'Living in Nairn, tutoring, helping on a friend's farm'.

*War and After*

Then war came. Olive Fraser was thirty years old and being unattached was liable for national service. The c.v. gives '1940, January to September, working on a friend's farm'. In April she applied for a post in the cypher department of the Royal Navy, W.R.N.S. and was accepted.

The official record of her service reads:

> September 1940: Two weeks officers' training course at R.N. College, Greenwich.

October/November 1940: Two weeks cypher training in Aberdeen.
November–April 1940–41: Employed on the staff of the Commander-in-Chief H.M.S. Cochrane II Rosyth and Western Approaches, Naval Intelligence Department.
May 1941: Appointment in W.R.N.S. terminated at own request. Rank IIIrd Officer WRNS.

Her own curriculum runs:
May 15, 1941: Was transferred to the Naval Intelligence Department of the Admiralty.
August 11, 1942: Compassionate release granted on account of my family's greatly increased ill-health.
Until about August 1946: At home in Nairn; helping a friend run her farm. Landgirl.

She had enjoyed the first taste of comradeship at Greenwich, as some effervescent fun-verses show ('O Grenovicia . . .') but very soon she was in the front line of conflict, the bombardment and aerial attack on the docks and harbours. When the blitz struck Merseyside one night in March 1941, then on the 3rd, 4th, 5th, 6th and 8th of May 1941, she was a junior officer on watch in Liverpool Docks. What was destroyed in her that night or fearful succession of nights, as human being and as poet, is to be found in her poetry, in poems like 'The Sleeper', 'After War' and 'In a Glen Garden'.

Of course no information can be asked from official sources as to why she left the service. And the Admiralty kept no record of temporary civil servants such as she became. A faint word of rumour has it that 'she went out of her mind after the maternity hospital near the docks was blitzed' . . . 'She thought the enemy were after her, trying to get in touch with her.' Certainly the damage wrought in her mind and personality went deep, witness the inner argument of the 'after war' poems and the submerged images of cowardice in the landgirl lyrics, light verses though they are.

In 1944 the beloved great-aunt died, after suffering grievously from cancer. Jottings among her literary papers show that Olive was nursing her with devotion, if with an amateur hand. Not long after that the lovely old house, Redburn, was given up. Olive's mother was received into an old people's home in Nairn, 'Whinnieknowe', where she lived to the end of her days. And about the same time Olive's beloved Irish terrier Quip died at a ripe old age. He is celebrated as devoted friend in a group of delightful epitaphs.

From this point on Olive had no home in the north or indeed anywhere. Her loss of the loved person and the loved place comes poignantly in a poem of 1946, 'The Empty House'. This is one of the earliest in a series of lyrics she was to write, year by year, as a 'mind' for the old highland lady who was her love, lamp, light, home, fireside and star. She may call her 'A.M.J.', 'Andrea', 'Anthea' or simply 'my love'.

In the summer of 1945 Olive made a bid to start afresh elsewhere. For a year she worked at Court House Farm, Great Coxwell near Faringdon in Berkshire taking charge of the poultry—and enjoyed it. In summer 1946 she attempted to approach once more her earlier world of learning, training as librarian's assistant in Bedford then attaining a post, though a humble one, in the Bodleian Library, Oxford.

Of Oxford she had high hopes—to be again in a university city of towers and spires, bells and ancient trees. Indeed she found congenial company there. Some were old friends. James Wyllie, with whom she had shared a desk in a wartime research department, was editing the *Oxford Latin Dictionary*. Oliver Zangwill from Cambridge days, now in the Institute of Experimental Psychology, with his wife Joy welcomed her when she first came. Later, lodging in the Woodstock Road she made new friends, among them the two Pasternak ladies, who remember her with affection. (Lydia was in touch with her by letter until Olive's death in 1977.) Among the Scots in Oxford was the redoubtable Scottish Nationalist Mrs Nannie K. Wells, herself a writer of verse and a meeting-point for kindred spirits. And Olive had a number of Catholic friends met in church.

To be in Oxford should have proved propitious for writing. Of the tally of poems that bear date or place of writing, more than thirty belong to the years 1945 to 1949, Berkshire, Bedford, Oxford. Some look back on the past, to war personalities or personal loss. One, on the ship Skidbladnir, 'To a Ship', links 'The Vikings' of 1935 to the poetry of northern Scotland that was to come. A new appearance is poetry of wild creatures as victims, the osprey and the cygnet, published here as 'On a Stoned and Dying Cygnet'. She copied out the title many times (and as often changed her mind about the wording), leaving a doubt as to whether the cygnet died from a parent-bird's attack or from subsequent stoning by the hand of man. The issue was one she took fiercely to heart. In these years the tone of the writing is sombre.

Most unfortunately Olive Fraser's employment in the Bodleian Library ended in disaster. As a Cambridge graduate she was allowed a reader's ticket and could browse at will in her free time, but she was engaged as a librarian's assistant doing a job a girl out of school could do and might do better. In the end this rankled, a clash of personalities developed and a sad and sorry row meant that she resigned in rage and high dudgeon.

This we gather from papers she was careful to keep. One of these was a draft letter to Father Wheeler, who was at that time Chaplain to Catholic students of the University of London. This contact suggests that Olive may not entirely have given up hope of continuing work on her thesis begun in 1935, on the use of the Bible by seventeenth–century poets, perhaps with the idea of linking her studies to one of the Colleges in London. However that may be, sometime in 1949 she did finally abandon the research scheme, witness the harrowing epitaph 'The Unwritten Book'.

> She sits, long mummified, upon her stool
> The goddess, in some pantry of my soul.
> 'My God', I say, 'she shall sit there no more!'
> And drag her, flaming, frantic, through the door.

## Greenwich

In 1949 she moved to London, to Greenwich, which she had come to know in her first days in the WRNS. Greenwich she loved, finding there an entity she could be happy to live in, as she had been happy in Old Aberdeen: a characterful township, steeped in history and story, with fine ancient buildings and old, huge trees, within the smell of the tides and the sight of a ship, a heath not far off and parkland at the street's end.

After lodging a while at 9, Stockwell Street, an address now demolished, she took over from summer 1951 one of a terrace of old little houses, 77, Royal Hill. These are now desirable residences since Greenwich refurbished itself in 1977 for the royal Jubilee year, but then they were dejected and near-derelict. Her next-door neighbour of those days is still there and remembered: 'She took over when the two old ladies moved out. Took over their sticks of furniture, too. No hot water or anything like that . . .' On this home she looks back with affection in a letter she wrote many years later:

Bennachie,
[Cornhill Hospital, Aberdeen]
7 December, 1974.

Dear Elma,
. . . It was a real cottage, which I once inhabited for 6½ years. Like all the rest of my life, my habitation there was chequered, yet I had many happy hours there. I don't think my friends would call them happy—but they were. I had a large stew-pan, without a handle, with a gorgeous white tobacco plant growing in it, and I used to take this in at night to scent my tiny study—it smelt like a tropical forest. I can't think of any of my friends who would approve, except my friend who is a Franciscan friar, but I feel St Francis of Assisi would understand and, feeling this, I do not care what anyone else says about my atrocious poverty. There were no fitted carpets, no revolving book-cases or elegant units—I had made most of the furniture myself, being employed by a firm that had its own saw-mill and was very generous in a thoughtful, kindly way to its employees and even to people who lived around. I used to get all sorts of goods from this firm that were only for export and for sale at bargain prices to its own employees!

Love,
Olive

Details in the poems of the poet and the poet's house, 'the rag-stuffed pane', 'a heartless room', were all too near the truth.

In the summer of 1951, then, Olive Fraser set up in the only home she was to make for herself in her whole life. The set determination to devote the best of her mind and time to poetry meant that she would only work part-time or for part of the time—every day for a spell or full time on some menial job quite decently paid, then a spell off. She had little sense of physical comfort and her housekeeping

14

was sketchy, but in that she may not be substantially different from many women scholars at that time: impractical, used to lodgings or a college room, totally unprepared for the emergencies of maintaining the roof, a door, a supply of fuel or something in the larder.

This pattern of life served well enough by the poet's own standards. But in 1951, the year of the Scottish contest, she was reported to be penniless and in poor health. This we know because an urgent appeal was made on her behalf for the prizemoney due to her to be paid over without further delay. The appeal was made by Father Alexander Burgess, who was a Franciscan of the Order of Minor Capuchins of Erith, a few miles further down the Thames. The Franciscans were hospital visitors for the area and it was possibly in this capacity that Olive had made their acquaintance. There is an unexplained, undated period in 'St Francis Hospital, East Dulwich' (a mental hospital) where she wrote 'To Poetry': 'Follow, my ghost, unto the hills of gold . . .' a lyric written in her earlier style. It is possible that Olive recuperated there after the breaking-point during the war, but subsequently wiped the interlude from her reckoning.

At all events by 1951 she was happily in touch with the brothers of Erith. One of them, who had 'a blessed Celtic presence', helped her over some crisis of eviction. A letter of thanks survives. It was possibly he who was of aid to her in her study of Gaelic. But the main friend and stay was Father Alexander, himself a Scot and writer of verse, and a considerable scholar conversant with the tradition of the mystics, with St Teresa of Avila and St John of the Cross.

For many years, in fact since her schooldays in Nairn, Olive had been going to the services of the Catholic Church—this in defiance of active opposition from her family who were Presbyterians. Now she seriously wished to be received into it and Father Alexander was her instructor. A page of prose entitled 'The Open Door' enjoyed a prominent place among her assembled papers; it was possibly an exercise written during instruction and describes vividly her gradual moving from Presbyterian childhood towards Catholicism. (It is printed in *The Tablet,* 1st September, 1984 in 'A Poet Rediscovered'.) In the summer of 1952 she was received into the Church.

The autumn of that year was marked also by the death of her father, Roderick Fraser, at the age of 72, in Aberdeen, after half a lifetime of invalidism in the home of his sister Elizabeth; she was the wife of William McDougall, a substantial merchant in Aberdeen, who had a corner shop at Gilcomston Steps. Roderick Fraser died intestate but there may have been a little money for his daughter. Or there may not.

Within the twelvemonth 1951 to 1952 someone else died who was near to Olive Fraser, someone belonging to the world of ships, sea-faring or the navy and suffering severely from the aftermath of war. 'After War', 'Thou no more dost seek the ghost . . .' laments his passing, which is remembered twenty years later on Hallowe'en 1971 in 'The Locked Door', 'Through all the dark fields of absence I love you yet.' The 'friend of whom I never speak' remains unknown, but the delight in his company and the shock of his death resound in the poetry in the recurring image of the shut door.

Meanwhile, though she was writing poetry and life had some happiness in it, the chosen pattern of work was wearing thin. By 1953 the nearest employment exchange found it well nigh impossible to direct Olive Fraser to any vacancy she was likely to find feasible or for which she was liable to be accepted, if she made the effort to hasten to it and present herself. After a series of attempts that miscarried or had been mismanaged, the Labour Exchange refused to continue her unemployment assistance. Outraged, she took them to court. Some of the documents survive, including the wrong-headed but eloquent letter she wrote in her defence. (She apparently did not appear in person.)

The record of her employment since the end of 1950 ran thus:

National Insurance Number K M 74 93 66

9 weeks, 13.11.50–26.1.51: Librarian, Grayladies College, Dartmouth Row, Greenwich.

1 year, 26.6.51–July 1952: 'Soldering', Peak Frean and Co, Bermondsey.

4 days, 21.12.52–24.12.52: Assistant nurse, L.C.C. Ladywell, Lewisham.

3 weeks, 2.7.53–24.7.53: Clerical, Sabels, Great Clyde Street, S.E. London.

Ill health, including bronchitis, had undermined her looks, her energy and initiative. Poor nutrition may have played a part. Poverty had reduced her to shabbiness. 'I've had but the one new outfit

16

in the last twelve years' she said in 1953. By 'new outfit' a Scot of Olive's generation would mean a coat-and-skirt or an overcoat of substantial tweed, durable for a decade—such as Olive had always worn at college . . . In an application to Goldsmith's College (to the library), Lewisham Way, S.E.4, she was judged unsuitable to serve as a counter hand. What was the ultimate outcome of the proceedings is by no means clear. The anguish entailed is manifest. The case was tried on 11 November 1953. Deptford—The Proceedings of the Local Tribunal, 9/19 Rushey Green, Catford, S.E.6.

The record of employment cited above begins just when entries were due for the poetic contest in Scotland. Because of Father Alexander's appeal for the prize-money—£40 and £20—to be paid, the poet's straitened circumstances became known in the north, in particular to the editor of *The Mercat Cross,* a family magazine published in Edinburgh by the Jesuit Order. Father Ronald Moffatt S.J. edited it until 1957 and was happy to recall his acquaintance with Olive. 'I encouraged and was happy to publish the poems of an obviously gifted writer'. The poems printed in *Temenos* in 1988, as he says in a letter to me, 'brought back the threnody sound of her verses as we heard them unforgettably in that Christmas Number of The Mercat Cross when she was spread across the central pages. It is an unmistakable voice and though I spoke about threnody there is a kind of heavenly philosophy that touches her verse to a warm glow.' (6th June, 1988)

By the year 1954, just after the desperate and exhausting bout with officialdom, things seem to be going more easily. One mode of journalism that brought in a little money was the letter to the newspaper. She joined in a controversy in *The Sunday Times* on 'Which six books would you give up a meal to possess?' Several letters were published. Her list reads: I would sacrifice a meal for *Prayer and Poetry* by Abbé Henri Brémond, *Diary of a Country Priest* by George Bernanos, *Under Milk Wood* by Dylan Thomas, *Arrows* by Sir Alexander Gray, *Two Quiet Lives* by Lord David Cecil and *The Life of Mehitabel by Archie the Cockroach*—Don Marquis'. And the first of these, she said, she would tramp the roads penniless to possess.

The same year, 1954, saw Olive gathering her poems together with the idea of publishing a collection. Mrs Wells, her friend in Oxford, had encouraged her in this. (A list of thirty-eight titles exists marked 'for N.K.W.'). How far the project got is difficult to tell. On discovering that Mrs Wells planned to publish her own verses and Olive's together, Olive blew up. The project was not heard of again; but the list of titles is some help in dating the poems as 'by 1954'. Another attempt was the preparation of a 'Book of Poetry' written into a brown-leaved drawing-book in Olive's best script (which could be beautiful). This has items marked 'for Father C', which is probably Father Philip Caraman, one time editor of *The Month*.

Despite disappointments, her poems one by one were finding their way into print. One lyric 'Beauty of Bethlehem' and perhaps others, she placed with a periodical in America (which I have not traced). 'The American dollars' were slow in coming and in despair Olive wrote to Sir Alexander Gray asking for temporary aid. He was happy to send her £15 to tide her over—but expressed anxiety about her scheme of life and work.

The year 1955 must have been a bleak one. A black one too. Not a ray of light can be shed on its course.

## In Hospital, London, and Recovering in the North

The onset of severe mental illness in 1956 was apparently sudden. We have word of it from a friend, who recalls walking in London with Olive in 1957 and suggesting they go into the big Forte's restaurant at the corner for a cup of tea. Olive flinched and registered strong alarm. 'No,' she said. 'That's where I was working when I fell ill. I was walking along and I just blacked out and when I came to, I found myself up a tree.' In 1956 she was admitted to Bexley Hospital as a voluntary patient. The consultant who admitted her, very junior at the time, remembered her well, her 'rather beautiful rounded face.' He recalls that it was a most daunting experience for a young doctor to argue about what was normal behaviour and what abnormal with a formidable personality, a mind that could defend itself in such cogent speech. He became her very good friend in hospital.

From this time on she was under the care of Bexley Hospital, either in their wards or under the eye of an almoner. This was Mrs Nanice Avery, as Olive calls her in a letter, 'a blessed friend. After

I was home she would go a mile out of her way at night to see that I was all right and had a fire.' The occupational therapist Lalage Dawson-Jones was a kindred spirit in fun and witty phrase-making, and proved a friend for life. She herself was physically handicapped and Olive had a profound admiration for her courage, her beauty and charm. She volunteered to do fatigues—to help her move heavy files in her office and run errands for her, jesting, 'I only do it in order to cadge a cup of tea!'

Another congenial contact in hospital was Mrs Pat Thurston, who helped run the art-classes. Her husband, Martin Thurston, was art-editor of *The Croydon Advertiser,* a daily newspaper that ran an intelligent art-and-literature page once a week. Here Olive found, over the years, an outlet for now a lyric, now an article. (As late as 1976 she sent him a handful of poems, among them 'The Dream Castle' which she had just written.)

A pattern has now begun that was to weave for the rest of her life: in and out of hospital. There were to be long stretches of gray, crises of danger, desperation and suffering—but all against a lasting web of friendships, maintained through all difficulties in live contacts and visits, in letters and laughter exchanged.

The first spell in hospital lasted eight months. She was writing, both in hospital and out of it. Not long afterwards a lucky thing occurred. She was on a visit to friends in Oxford. In Oxford also that spring of 1957 was a young Norwegian scholar, Rolf Karlsen, preparing his thesis for Bergen University on English language. He had asked James Wyllie if he could recommend a scholar in the field with some time to spare who would check through his style and usage as his work progressed. Wyllie recommended Olive. The project prospered. Karlsen moved to London for the summer and he and Olive met frequently to discuss points at issue. They used to talk over a meal in the Scandinavian Seamen's Restaurant or relaxing in a teashop after tea. I asked him how Olive seemed in health. In the year he met her she 'seemed like someone who has been very ill but is, say, 75% recovered. On one occasion Olive passed her hand over her forehead and said: "Oh dear! I haven't felt very well for the last few days. I must see my doctor."'

On one occasion only did he come to visit her. In 1957 he and James Wyllie made the trip to Greenwich by water. They were entertained to lunch at Grayladies' College, where Deaconess Lister, ever a friend to Olive, laid on a meal for them. They had tea at 77 Royal Hill, where the humble dereliction filled him with disquiet. Karlsen's second visit to London in the summer of 1959 saw a happy resumption of this scholarly consultation. (It had continued through letters in the interim.) Olive still went up from Greenwich for the meetings in London. Part of the summer it was from Bexley Hospital that she came, but she did not say so. After his return to Norway he kept up the connection, sending her chapters to overlook. He and his wife remembered her generously every Christmas, with a parcel of delicious eatables—and two splendid brightly-coloured woollen ski-jackets. Olive preferred to be recompensed in kind: wearing the brilliant jerseys boosted her morale in hospital.

After the eight months in 1956 'when I first had a break-down' Olive was back living in Royal Hill, with kind friendship and support from, among others, Deaconess Lister of Greyladies College Dartmouth Row 'just up the hill'. Though from 1957 she was working with Karlsen, she does not appear to be writing poetry.

In 1958 she was in hospital for a month during April and May. Writing to Karlsen she made light of it: she had known for some time she was going to be admitted without knowing when; she was not ill—she had plenty of leisure. By May 30 she was back home. But on July 1 she was again in Bexley Hospital, Dr Tait having said he did not wish her to go back to live in Greenwich. She remained in hospital for nine months, depressed and distressed. Deaconess Lister went to see her and reported her to be far from well. (Karlsen kept in touch with Deaconess Lister out of anxiety about their friend. The information above comes from correspondence between him and the poet.)

Comments made to the doctors taken from hospital records bear this out, for instance 13 August 1958—'I will never write again and might as well be dead.' On 5 September she was worried about her two gold medals which she had pawned years ago in Aberdeen, and told the doctor. (Father Burgess thereupon arranged for them to be rescued.) Yet in October she writes to Karlsen: 'I am not ill. I just cannot write any literature and am worried about it. It is as though I had lost a limb.' Writing to Karlsen who is far away, she is as ever anxious to save face.

In November she went for a week-end to the Averys. In December, suffering from bronchitis, she was packing the contents of her cottage for storage. After the giving-up of 77 Royal Hill it is good to learn that, at a Christmas party at Grayladies she is reported as 'being very lively company.' Early in 1959 in hospital she is still maintaining 'I am unable to write, but I was a writer. I will never write again'. She wonders—is it the illness or the drugs?

In the spring of 1959 Olive made another effort to live in the world outside. A series of addresses shows her way of life to be unsettled. In June her aged landlady died and in her next lodgings Olive fell ill with bad influenza and bronchitis and reached the depths; in January 1960 she was admitted to hospital in a coma after a heavy overdose of drugs. Her landlady would not have her back so she was homeless. This time she stayed in hospital for over a year.

21 January 1960: 'I am not what I was. Since my breakdown in '56 I am working on a 5%–10% of my personality. When I take drugs and feel better then I say I am working or thinking in terms of 50%–60% of my personality. I was a Roman Catholic but I left because I saw the political influence of the Church. I was a writer. I cannot write now.' (Quotations from hospital records made for me by Dr A. C. Smith.)

Olive's reaction to the medication she received in hospital is seldom enthusiastic. That now one treatment now another was being tried to see what might best help her she neither realised nor acknowledged. At a much later point, writing to Karlsen, she says that at Bexley Hospital she had been given ritalin which made her feel energetic but did not combat her inability to write. When she was prescribed chlorpromazine she says she felt as if she had been 'hammered down in a box and dropped below the Bermuda Deep'; but during this time a couple of lyrics did get written, admittedly unserious ones. At the time the doctors commented: 'She is idle. She does her stint of dusting but otherwise sits curled up in an armchair smoking and reading.'

The despair she felt at not being fully in command of her own intellect—of not having access to it, of having no spiritual existence is the worst affliction that is directly recorded in any document available to me. There is one frightening prose piece in her own papers which begins: 'My life has always been full of fear . . .' and goes on to expound this in a mingle of fantasy and verifiable fact. It appears to have been written for the doctors.

What we do not have—in any writing I have access to—is any

trace of her main terror—of the voices she heard. One pregnant sentence in the account she wrote as a newspaper article about her life at Bexley Hospital lets us know: 'I heard no more voices now.' In the masterly poems of 1964 'Lines Written After a Nervous Breakdown' we can glimpse the nature of the terrors experienced in 'this/ Inevitable mind's abyss'. Later, in the seventies in Cornhill Hospital in Aberdeen, Olive most carefully avoided contact with any patient who 'heard voices'—as I was told by Miss Cook, occupational therapist there and Olive's loyal friend. For a poet who awaited with reverence the arrival of 'the visitor' who was inspiration, for a writer engaged over a writing lifetime in a colloquy within her mind, terror by voices heard within must have been the ultimate torture.

This precarious and partial overview is all that has been possible of Olive Fraser's time in Bexley Hospital, intermittently from 1956 to 1961—my amateur collation of matter from disparate sources. The letters to Professor Karlsen are full and vivid but it has to be remembered that Olive was writing to an academic colleague abroad and was anxious at all points to save face. I had a kind communication from Dr Tait who treated her and happy and helpful talks with Nanice Avery and with Lalage Dawson-Jones, who lent me letters. I was lucky too to have the unstinting help of Dr Andrew C. Smith, who was a consultant in Bexley Hospital when I began my enquiry. He was working on a book *Schizophrenia and Madness*, (since published), and took up the investigation of the poet-patient with enthusiasm. Her poetry he found of the greatest interest especially the two 'Lines . . .' on recovering. (He used stanzas from 'Lines I' as epigraph to his book. It was he who, while searching the archives at my request, came upon the two wonderful lyrics 'When I shall die . . .' and 'Where is now my happy Harp?' which Olive sent to the doctors with the defiant message interleaved. Alas that Dr Smith fell severely ill and died and that the project we had planned, of studying 'the schizophrenic who wrote poetry', was not to be.

Towards the end of 1960 Olive began to feel the pull of the north—'hamedracht'. Her deep-seated discontents suggested to her that at least one cause of them was living in London. She was now dreaming of returning to Scotland to live, where she would be able to visit her mother, where she belonged. Olive though improvident had the capacity to 'save up' for something she really wanted. (She was a habitual saver-up of cigarette coupons for gifts.) Now she joined a work-scheme the hospital was running for modest cash reward. Stuffing teddybears. She toiled at it, but found the discipline of organised labour as ruinous as the aching of back-muscles unaccustomed to hard work with the hands. Nevertheless her dream slowly became a possibility. She was in herself much better and longed to begin life afresh and in new surroundings.

In 1961, in the spring, Olive reached her ambition. She discharged herself from Bexley Hospital and made for the north. She left a warm circle of friends and well-wishers and had many farewell gifts and envelopes to open in the train. She had decided to live in Inverness, perhaps at the suggestion of the Hospital, as support would not be far away—in Craig Dunain Hospital. They put her in touch with doctors and she knew a friend who would be willing to take her in. There she would be able to see her mother often, in Nairn only a short journey away by bus or train. She was taking her life into her own hands—and she relished the fact—though not without misgivings. But she knew few people in Inverness itself and had not realised how much she had counted on the web of friendships in London. She was lonely and scared. Not an easy housemate, she moved from address to address. Timorous, understandably after hospitalisation, feckless by nature and reckless by character—that was one risk too many. She soon fell ill again and entered Craig Dunain.

It was only at this point that her whereabouts, her presence in the north, became known to old college friends resident in Aberdeen. Someone visiting there had glimpsed her in the grounds of Craig Dunain, striding past, clutching a battered typewriter. She was in hospital for nearly two years—and found it 'very old-fashioned, compared to London'. After some months as an outpatient she was sent to Edinburgh for a training course in typing. She still manfully maintained that she was looking for a job.

In 1963 she made up her mind to return to Aberdeen to live, where she had been happy as a student and would find a number of friends from student days. She was encouraged in making another bid to live in the outside world by Ian Begg, a friend from childhood, now Episcopalian Bishop of Aberdeen and Orkney. At this time he was prominent as a supporter of the 'back into the community' movement for hospital patients. He found her lodgings in the

Altoun (Old Aberdeen), a place Olive loved. But with Olive this was not a success. Things quickly went very wrong and she was on the move again, from one emergency address to another. She was, of course, in touch with the mental hospital—The Royal Cornhill Hospital and was attending the Ross Clinic. She was fond of her G.P., a contemporary from her days at King's though she had not known him then. 'Jimmy Third,' she wrote, 'treats me like a human being. When I go to wail to him he gives me a glass of sherry.'

From 1963 she found lodgings very near to Cornhill Hospital in 9, Ashgrove Road, in the very house where her chum Jean Sinclair had lodged in student days. Here my sister Elma R. Mennie sought her out—and from this point on her story leaves the dimnesses of memory, rumour or chance meeting and enters the common daylight of visits and exchange of letters. Olive's letters my sister fortunately kept, and the poems she often included. In Ashgrove Road she occupied 'the little room over the front door' which belonged to the constant pattern of the granite dwelling-houses of Aberdeen. For the most part she kept the blinds down as the seda-tive medicine she was taking rendered her oversensitive to sunlight. There were piles of old women's magazines on the floor: she made a habit of entering competitions in them which often turned on writ-ing an effective jingle, and she determinedly sent them short stories for publication. Texts of some of these survive and they are imagi-native and fantastical, largely recreations of her childhood hours or projections of her own anxieties (the gifted orphan child misused is a frequent figure). But for that readership she was shooting wildly off target. She had more success with newspaper articles—and here her old connections were of use still. *The Croydon Advertiser* printed her article on hospital life 'The House Where You May Cry' in summer 1964, and others later on.

Her housekeeping was primitive and erratic. 'She hadna even a teapot!' lamented a Jeans relative who looked her up when visiting the north. Writing she was, and with determination; but if there are poems from the years 1958 to 1964 they cannot definitely be dated. From several quarters come the repeated words 'I am being given valium. I cannot write poetry.' Suddenly in a flash come two superb poems, a pair with the same title 'Lines written after a nervous breakdown I and II'.

The eccentricity of her home-life worried Olive far less than it worried her friends. Her housekeeping lurched along at this subsistence level helped by many kind hands—the Legion of Mary or certain wellwishing citizens met at church or at the Newman Society, who realised only gradually the predictableness of disaster in her fortunes. An official visitor with hospital connections might be horrified at the outset, but would succumb to volatile spirits, spell-binding conversation and a bond, tacit and conspiratorial, to laugh it all off as unimportant. On the other hand, someone who had known her in college days, informed of her plight, might look her up bringing a companion. While the fellow-student of old was simply horrified, the new acquaintance might be intrigued by Olive's conversation, impressed by her will to happiness and wish to make friends—only to be discreetly advised not to take matters farther or 'you'll have her *always* on your doorstep.' This is the inside-out of such bitter and penetrating poems as 'On the Virtue of a Single Meeting'.

Of the friends she made at the Newman Society the principal ones were the Stamms. Betty taught at a Catholic primary school—she was a highland Scot from Tomintoul. Roman her husband, a Polish exile, an ex-marine of war-wrecked physique, worked as gardener at Blairs College. Olive made friends in 1965. They were but recently married and lived in a picturesque old cottage in the depths of the country near Blairs. During Olive's years of friendship with them they had a child, Marysia, to their great happiness as older parents.

Inclusion in this family circle gave Olive wonderful hours of happiness; it breathes in the poetry—'The Fire of Apple Wood', 'To Roman Stamm'. They were cat-lovers as she was and round their cat Mihailovicz Olive wove an epic of adventures. Her daft streak of humour chimed with theirs and Olive stood godmother to the baby girl.

With friends in the south she kept in touch by regular exchange of letters: Lalage Dawson-Jones and Nanice Avery, Pat and Martin Thurston. Several of them made the journey once to Aberdeen to see her. They would invite her down to visit them in London, often helping with the fare. My sister Elma Mennie came north to Aberdeen from time to time. She knew Olive found pleasure in the simplest delights, walking over airy moorland heights or sitting by a burnside watching the birds and the rising trout. She would drive her out to the Deeside hills or to the sea. On a day of anguish or low spirits they would walk and talk in the gracious setting of the Cornhill grounds or retire to Olive's own domain, her 'room up the long stair' (her expression) to chat and tease and reminisce. Davidina and Ronald Garden, both friends from her King's College days would receive her into their home in Aberdeen at whatever inconvenient hour she might call. A fine poem shows her dependence on such faithful friends for defence against desperate thoughts: 'To Dinah and Ronnie Garden—at Night'.

In summer 1964 Olive's mother died. The fierce impact this made on her has been recorded in a letter.

9 Ashgrove Road
Aberdeen
18 September, 1965.

Dear Elma,

I am awfully sorry you arrived when I was feeling so sick and the place like a pigsty, as I had not done any washing-up over the weekend, being out with Jean Boylan. However it was better your arriving then than the next Monday when I awoke in panic and shivered with fear the whole day until I crept down to the bus at night and went to my doctor, who said it was just reaction after Mother's death . . . Mondays seem to produce a crisis, as last Monday I did what I have not done for nine years [i.e. since 1956 and her first breakdown] . . . burst into tears and could not stop for hours . . . Anyway after the Monday I spent in stark terror I made up my mind that I am not staying here but probably going back to London . . .

Olive

Recuperation took some little time. A year later she wrote to Helena M. Stuart who had been a fellow-student at King's and now offered sympathetic friendship, the more so in that she herself had known mental trouble.

9 Ashgrove Road,
Aberdeen,
7th September 1966

Dear Lena,

Here is the Prayer to the Virgin I wrote so many years ago, which was published in America and which has now been set to music. I heard the music on the cathedral organ after High Mass on Sunday—it sounded simply beautiful. I thought you would like a copy as you have been so good to me.

I am better now and have written a poem, thanks to Dr Third. And you. He said it was emotional shock. I have heard from Nanice Avery who wants me down next summer. So does Deaconess Lister.

I have been having more letters from Father Alexander and more music. I shall enclose one called 'The Church' which has been set to music. Needless to say, I was not in these days the worthless person I am now. I was seven-eighths starved, but I was happy. Father Alexander was instructing me, and he used to feed me with bars of chocolate and cups of coffee during instructions. He ceases to be Guardian of his monastery on the 13th of this month and will be sent somewhere else. How blessed I am to have him for a friend.

Yours sincerely,
Olive Fraser

Father Alexander Burgess had the happy idea of 'collecting' a number of lyrics by Olive Fraser and having them set to music for voice and piano by a fellow Franciscan, Father Leo Rowlands. These settings Olive kept among her papers. The lyrics set are 'The Church' 'She is a ship . . .', 'The Blessed Ones' 'The poor hawks of the mountains', 'The Poet (V)' 'When shall I come to Thy Abode', 'Prayer to the Virgin' 'O Bethlehem . . .' and 'Invocation to Our Lady' 'Thou above my heart'.

In 1966 Olive was treated in hospital for a period of several months. She reports to Karlsen, writing for Christmas, 'I am very well, better than I have been for years, thanks to the ministrations of a splendid hospital down the road. I had a shadow on my lung and while I was there for four months the doctor took me off the drug I had used to have. It made the most tremendous difference.

27

I hadn't really been well since I had that nervous breakdown I had before I met you (1956). Now I am in robust health—it was at least partly the drug I had been ordered that was making me ill.'

In the later sixties, then, Olive speaks of being able to write again and of feeling somewhat better. Indeed a number of poems among the many in her papers that bear no note of date or place may belong to these years leading up to 1970. But there is no saying for sure. The exchange of letters with Karlsen ceases after Christmas 1967, barring a note at Christmas 1968. There she gives her address as 'Elmhill, Cornhill Hospital' but explains it away: she could write no letters as she had no digs—she is staying in this hospital where she knows one of the doctors until she manages—she hopes—to get a cottage somewhere . . . Unfortunately the series of letters to Elma Mennie are, with one exception, preserved only from September 1970. And Olive's own retyping and ordering of her poems, undertaken systematically in her later years, works backward in time, reaching 1970 but no earlier. On internal evidence of subject matter and style I should place about a score of the undated poems as belonging to the later sixties. These resemble the poems for Lena Stuart and show experiment in lyrics without end-rhyme and in longer lines whose rhythm is relaxed. Some are good but none is compelling.

## The 'Wonderful Years', Aberdeen: Hospital and Holidays

Some time in late 1968 Olive had been ill again, suffering from bronchitis. She was persuaded by Dr Helen MacLean to come into Cornhill Hospital for a spell to be looked after. Dr MacLean, who had been in touch with her for some time, had diagnosed her case as hypothyroidism, myxoedema, and had decided to combat it by dosing her with thyroxin, but for this Olive must be in hospital so that dosage and administering could be fully monitored. Olive's condition improved quickly and dramatically. Elma Mennie, who as a schoolgirl had known her in the thirties and had been her loyal friend since 1963, bears witness to the astonishing transformation. Between visits to her three months apart Olive had lost weight dramatically. From overheavy build and shapeless form she had got back to 'her own size in slips'. Her tough and hardened skin had cleared, her eyes had their old look of penetrating blue, and her hair, of which she had been 'inordinate proud' in youth and which had been a dire casualty of her condition, was coming back to its sheen and colour.

A letter dated 23rd June 1970 thanks for the gift of a nice jumper. 'I have lost almost three stones but your dresses look fine on me. I am taking them south for the holiday with Nanice Avery.'

Thereafter begin 'the three wonderful years of good health' she speaks of with thankfulness, again and again. With return of health and wellbeing, restitution of personable appearance and the happiness that brought with it, came a flood of creative writing. Comments from her letters make sad but happy reading. This to Elma Mennie is dated 27th June, 1973.

Dearest Em,

I haven't felt so well since before I went to Cambridge —have 22 pills a day, but most thankful for them.

Look after yourself. I am just having a cup of tea before going to bed.

No. I have never contacted the *Guardian*. I still write poetry, however. I feel that you and all your friends walk in a world I shall never know. I had such disfigurement for so long with this thyroid thing that even my own friends used to upbraid me for it, although I couldn't help it. They, and strangers, made it worse than it was. It gives me a wry feeling when people say to me now 'what beautiful hair you have' (I spend 2–3 minutes a day on it, and when I spent three hours desperately on my crow's nest growth as it was then they said to me exasperatedly, 'Why do you never comb your hair?') This did me an awful lot of harm—the symptoms were really worse than the illness, swollen lips, puffy eyes (for which they gave me medicated soap and penicillin ointment) and a brown-grey leathery skin. All gone now.

Well, ducky doodle, look after yourself. Cosset yourself. Remember the text goes 'Love thy neighbour *as thyself*.' Now, on this hortatory note I will close. Saved up enough coupons to get a travelling clock from Players—expected next week—but had to buy the last 400 as their catalogue is on the point of changing.

Much love,
Olive
. . . Oystercatchers have a fine handsome family in a field at the back.

29

Inside Cornhill Hospital she had firm friends also. The occupational therapist Miss Agnes Cook, the charge-nurse Alan Fowlie, a young nurse from Germany Christa Ahrens and her friend Meg Myles who was a librarian. These two much younger women would include her now and then in a merrymake, a meal in a Chinese restaurant or such. And one summer they took her with them in the 'van' as far north as Sutherland. This was bliss indeed—and out of that journey poem after poem was born.

Olive never tried again to weather life in the world outside. She was now close on sixty years of age and in hospital she had found a way of life. From 1968 she writes from 'Elmhill, Cornhill Hospital'. From October 1971 she writes from 'Bennachie', a hill-top address she must have found congenial: in this building within the grounds she had a little upstairs room all to herself, an eyrie approached by a steep service-stair. There she could write and read and look out on the tree-top birds and be at peace in a cosy mess of papers and books, typewriter and cups of tea. Her meals were there and her health was supervised. She was free to come and go, wander the streets of a town she loved, even make her way to its neighbouring sea-coast or countryside. One great sadness: early in 1970 Dr Helen MacLean died, suddenly. 'I have some very sad news. Our much loved and brilliant Deputy Physician Superintendant took a heart-attack in the small hours of Sunday morning and died. What this hospital is, was very much due to her. That was my one powerful friend here' (Letter to Elma R. Mennie)

The year of the following letter is not on record. It is probably 1972.

Bennachie,
Cornhill Hospital,
Easter Sunday

Postscript to a letter to E.R.M.
. . . Night-Sister Campbell has just been round. She has not seen me for a long time. She was exclaiming about my hair and my skin. Isn't it the very dickens to have gone about for 39 years, ²/₃ of one's life, looking like an old gnarled tree-trunk on the top of which a drunken crow had built an untidy nest, and now, when I have 1¾ feet in the grave, to have elegant hair and skin again! If I weren't

philosophic I could weep over all the sickness and langours of these 39 years, but when I think of the awful things which happened quite undeservedly to some of my old friends and acquaintances who had everything going for them, I don't. I'm just thankful to have my *health,* and, although it means taking 22 pills a day, what of it. So this Easter night, I sit in peace with the candle.

If I were never to have any more than these two years of good health that I have had, they have been worth it.

O

Hospital life for the poet-inmate was not without its dreadful hours, when the impact on her of disturbed patients, her daily companions, assaulted her mind and battered her spirit. One such patient at mealtimes would let loose a torrent of filthy abuse at table. Olive protested that it was intolerable, though the nurse countered: 'We have to stand it, Miss Fraser.' She insisted that it would destroy her and was allowed to take her meals in peace, alone in the pantry. Under these circumstances she wrote 'The Sanctuary' (also called 'The Kootenay Ram'). For solace her mind had gone back to childhood reading, to the pages of Ernest Thompson Seton—'Krag, the Kootenay Ram', the story of a ram of the threatened species in the Canadian Rockies. This wild ram, a noble creature with magnificent horns, was pursued season after season by the degenerate and mean-minded hunter Scottie, intent on the money a kill would bring. Finally he shot it down and over the dead body he let loose a flood of filthy abuse—in Scots. Olive Fraser under stress found her way to sanctuary in her mind's store of creative writing and devised a solace in poetry.

Many poignant encounters with fellow-patients are recorded in the wonderful 'hospital poetry' of the later years. She is one of them— through her consciousness as a poet she is able to express their feelings which cannot find outlet in words. Some poems cry out in protest on their behalf. At moments she herself could experience the impossibility of expressing a sympathy deeply felt—as in 'To A Friend Bereaved'. Here it was a young nurse who ran up to Olive sobbing, with a letter in her hand that told her her father was dead. Olive could find no word or gesture to comfort her—but later said it in poetry and gave the poem to the girl.

Poetry as solace—poetry that can 'minister to a mind diseased',

31

poetry as stored richness in the mind to have recourse to, or poetry to be written anew to make concord out of discord—the case of Olive Fraser bears witness to the concept, time-honoured if out of kelter with thinking today. She, suffering for years in hospital as a 'schizophrenic patient' put it this way: . . . 'I don't know how on earth I get my poetry written. My own girning is so deep-seated that I don't girn, because I should be a menace to end all menaces if I did. Fortunately my mind is split at about twelve different levels and the girning at one level becomes the grape-harvest of another as it gets channelled off . . .' (O.F. to E.R.M.: 6 December, 1971.)

The one deep hurt that even poetry could not cure was that inflicted by the 'unlove' of her parents. It set her on the long search for love that resounds in some of her finest poems—especially 'Desperate for Love'. Along with the search for love went the search for identity, which not only wrote itself into the poetry from early days but occupied much time and entailed anxious endeavour in her later years. She longed above all to possess proof on paper that Roderick Fraser had acknowledged her to be his daughter, 'child' of the marriage' and indeed with kind help from a lawyer friend she obtained copies of documents from Australia that would do this. But the same source made it clear to her that his behaviour to her mother had been scoundrelly indeed. Though her bond with her mother had never been close, she wrote in sorrow, in a letter to a lawyer friend . . . 'And she had been a beauty. She led the loneliest life and had no friends . . .' The roots of Olive Fraser's distress went very deep indeed. Small wonder that 'mistrust', 'misgivings', 'unsureness of myself' though they enabled her to write penetratingly on failures in human relationships, also penalised her in the realm of friendship itself.

Friendships for Olive Fraser supplied the place of the family network that belongs by right to a highland Scot but by separate strokes of sheer ill-luck was not there to catch her when misfortune struck. True, she had more distant relatives on the Jeans side, in this country or overseas, who made the journey to visit her but with none of them did she find she could form a lasting bond. (The missing first-cousins on the Fraser side, learning of her existence for the very first time some six years after her death, and hearing her story with sorrow, said independently of each other, 'If only we had known, we could have helped.') Olive valued each friendship so keenly that she kept her friends in separate pockets: she could not face the idea that they might talk her over. A past of mental illness breeds reticence and life in any institution fosters it.

Such anxious dependence on friends could put friendship itself at risk. It was one cause of a proneness to quarrel suddenly, often for no apparent reason and for ever. 'Mistrust', 'misgivings', 'unsureness' was another. She can say it in her poems, can indeed foresee the whole quarrel-sequence as well as the hurt and misery that would follow. Certainly out of these dearly valued friends, both men and women, who have been mentioned, four suddenly experienced this 'flist' of temper, offence taken over a chance word where no slight was intended. And once, in the case of Nanice Avery,—Mrs Avery never understood why—Olive, holidaying in her home in London in the early nineteen-seventies suddenly got to her feet and left and was never in touch again. The cause was simple—poverty.

However brave a face she put on 'my atrocious poverty' the hurt went very deep, that she had never been able to get out of the trap—of poverty, illness, incapacity to earn. 'Nobody will come, my love' holds the truth in its last line, 'Desperate, faithful poverty' where hope is inverted, faith is all too faithful and, instead of the 'charity' we expect comes 'poverty', like a slap in the face. Poverty is that without which charity would not be. The poem that follows is a scream of pain, defacing 'charity' with a discordant echo of one of the loveliest passages in the Bible: 'a sounding brass'. Suddenly she, with her considerable power of mind, could not bear it any more— having nothing, wearing other people's clothes, accepting always accepting kindnesses—and no way out ever.

The good years lasted until nearly 1975—and they *were* good years. She had friends in hospital and out, new and old, in Aberdeen and in the south. She had holidays, usually invited once a year by old friends in London. 1972 saw her revisiting Cambridge, when she lunched in King's College with Professor Oliver Zangwill, her friend of Cambridge days, now Professor of Experimental Psychology there. She renewed contacts in Berkshire and Oxford. Though she had those comings and goings with friends from the past she was becoming increasingly isolated in habit of mind. As Davidina Bonner, Mrs Garden, put it: 'After we had had a long thought or two about old times, and we had heard the latest

33

news of goings-on in the hospital there was very little to talk about; Olive was not in touch at all with current affairs, either in the city or in the world in general.' She said it herself in a poem:

A world that is lovely and free
A world that means nothing to me.

(unpublished)

She was conscious that this criticism was made. In a letter she countered:

I was never *with it* but that is maybe my saving grace, as I am very much 'with' other things (*vide* Linnaeus!) which fills my horizons with beauty.

(To E.R.M.: 29. October, 1973.)

The poetry she was writing can on occasion expound this very isolation. On the other hand many poems concern the process of remembering and the moments of vision it can bring. On several occasions she writes an after-thought to a lyric, an experience, of many years before. And, now in age herself, she writes a final, gentle farewell to her beloved great aunt. In the guaranteed peacefulness of being able to be by herself she writes some lovely poems of childhood, of youth seen through ageing eyes. And in that peace contemplation was possible. There now well up from underground sources of thought certain great issues that over decades had been present in the recesses of her mind. Certain inner journeys now reach an ending:

Bennachie
31st December 1974.

Dear Elma,
This Hogmanay is different. I am at peace and not miserable. I don't suppose I ever told you I shudder from the Lowland Hogmanay—at home in the Highlands we always kept the New Year as a religious festival. My mother's family had been Huguenots and preserved from generation to generation their old customs.

34

Very dignified, very quiet, somewhat solemn. I was appalled when I first met up with Hogmanay, and have remained shrinking from it.

But tonight is different. I went to the library through empty streets and changed my books. Then I returned and got a most unexpected Hogmanay gift, the first I have ever received. Then I washed my posh tray (Players') and put a plate in the middle of it and on the plate your wild lily candle, ready to light at five minutes to twelve.

Thank you very much for the kind gifts. I am just about to have one of your cigarettes and a cup of tea. I cannot get over not being shrouded in despair at Hogmanay.

I wish you a very happy and lucky 1975. You were looking grand.

Love
Olive

The good years lasted on into 1975 but that June brought severe and very painful phlebitis and she is 'most unwell', under treatment for it in Forresterhill Hospital until November. A handful of fine lyrics are written in 1976 despite an operation, major surgery for cancer of the bladder. A second operation followed in 1977 and in December of that year she died.

> I brought strange Algol with me
> And Betelgueuse . . .

Those were the two stars she had named in 'The Unwanted Child' where she saw herself as born under a two-fold influence, the two powers at conflict. Betelgeuse was bringer of all talents and honours—and she had the gift of poetry until almost the last of her days. Algol, the mischiefmaker, the most malevolent star in the heavens, had struck again and again through a strange lifetime.

Even after her death her story cannot be told to its end without the incidence of evil chance. Her funeral was planned for one day, but postponed in the hope that a relative could be found as next of kin to authorise cremation. But the earlier date had been named and friends assembled in severe weather—and waited in vain. When next day they assembled again it was the priest, due to say the requiem mass, who never arrived. In the depths of the country he had suffered a car accident on his way back from a distant christening. He

35

could not even get a message through—so in the end the Chaplain of the Hospital, a minister of the Kirk of Scotland, performed the funeral service. He spoke movingly of Olive Fraser, her courage in adversity and her gift of poetry.

## The Poetry

So far the lifestory has been told of a woman writer who courageously suffered mental illness and disfigurement over decades. Mental illness has certainly been the lot of many creative artists; in this she is in distinguished company indeed. The other affliction, hypothyroidism, most fortunately in her case did not stultify the mind, though it took cruel toll in other ways. The relation between creativity and certain types of madness has interested both doctors and critics. It will take an authority on the medical side—a doctor with an appreciation of scholarly poetry at that—to expound this fascinating case where the voice of the visiting muse modulates into the voices of delusion but also into the voice of 'the dearest guest of all', of Christ to the soul. Documents abound, both personal correspondence and the poems themselves.

What then of the poet? How her 'broken life' of everyday relates to the life of creative imagination she herself wonders in 'The Two Senses of Life' and in other fine lyrics. There is space here only to glance at the issue.

Olive Fraser died penniless in 1977 in the Royal Mental Hospital, Cornhill, Aberdeen in whose care she had been for many years. (Out of this hospital, too, came a long unopened packet of papers: the impressive life-writing of Christian Watt, an inmate there of earlier this century, a remarkable fisher-wife suffering from manic depression whose writings finally appeared as *The Christian Watt Papers* in 1983.) Inside the hospital Miss Fraser was known to be a poet. She would on request of her fellow-patients pen an ode, and an amusing one, for the retiral, say, of the hospital house-painter Tam McTavish. In gratitude for a kindness, such as a day's outing to the mountains

36

she loved, she might present a copy of a lyric she had just written. It was all she had to give. 'Poetry,' she would smile, 'I have reams of it. A book of poetry! But when I send a poem to a publisher with "Royal Mental Hospital" at the top they just grin. They don't even send the script back.' This was bitter for a writer whose poetry had won top prizes in two universities and had gained equal first for lyrics in Scots in a national contest alongside Alexander Scott and Sydney Goodsir Smith—and a prize for a Scots verse play.

Here is Olive Fraser's 'book of poetry' that no-one had been allowed to see. It is a treasure-house of surprises. The sound of her very individual voice, was known in the early nineteen-thirties to her fellow-students at King's College, Aberdeen—known again to a generation of undergraduates at Cambridge after she won the Chancellor's Medal. It sounded again in 1951 and 1952 when the prize-winning lyrics were printed in Edinburgh by Serif Books, and soon after, when the Jesuit monthly magazine of the Church *The Mercat Cross,* published in Edinburgh, featured several poems that at once became favourites: 'Benighted in the Cairngorms', 'The Glen of the Clearance', 'Beauty of Bethlehem' or her elegy for childhood playmates of Nairn who had been killed in war service at sea in 'Exmouth' or in 'Prince of Wales'. This elegy, printed first in *The Nairnshire Telegraph* went round the world, posted to 'children of Nairn' far overseas.

Then silence.

Later on a lyric of hers appeared from time to time in the pages of *The Aberdeen University Review.* In 1981, a year or two after her death, *The Pure Account,* a small selection gathered from texts in the hands of friends, came from Aberdeen University Press. Among some thirty lyrics there, a number stood out as of great distinction and were hailed as such by discriminating critics. A review of *The Pure Account* in *Lines Review* No 81 brought to light the lyrics of 1951, which were reprinted in *Lines* No 82. Then, in 1983, the bulk of her life's writing, her 'book of poetry' was fortunately retrieved—an inchoate mass of papers, some 400 lyrics in manuscript or typescript, drafts, versions, jottings, letters and memorabilia, going back to childhood and reaching to the last month of her life. Some were on exercise-book pages, some on paper bags, many stained with coffee-cup rings or cat footprints—a veritable hoard. Out of this treasury devotional lyrics of hers were printed in *The Tablet* and received with acclaim. And in 1988, *Temenos* 9 featured a group of her poems chosen by Kathleen Raine. The knotty problem of copyright that seriously impeded publication of this book is solved. Clearly the time is ripe for Olive Fraser's 'book of poetry' to appear.

Olive Fraser's writing of the forties and fifties before illness overtook her shows a strongly growing talent, poetry of a kind not to be found elsewhere. Lovely early lyrics apart, there are poems of war by a woman in uniform in the RN in Liverpool—and poems of 'after war', of anguish and guilt caused by her involvement in that destruction. As with her brother poet Ivor Gurney, 'after war' for her meant living in a mind that had broken under the strain. How few are the war-poems by women in Scotland and how few of these are written by combatants. In another vein she wrote a splendid 'Victory Ode', a frangible genre indeed as it passes down the years. But this poem calls out loudly what I and multitudes felt on that day, that the rivers were running clear again, the mountains clapping their hands.

Here are poems of devotion, both of the outer and inner life of religion, from celebrative poetry like the splendid 'On the Birth of Our Lady' (cosmic rejoicing at the birth of a baby *girl*) to the 'child poems' where a child's voice is speaking. The fierce and frightening 'The Poet to the Holy Ghost', written in hospital, is a prayer for deliverance from madness through the cleansing force of *creator spiritus,* who only can resolve inner confusion of mind through the gift of tongues. Also poignant and eloquently drawing on a great hymn of the early church is 'The Tree': here the poet speaks with the Cross itself, which is at once forest-tree for singing poet-bird and instrument of dire destruction. (Had she seen the picture *Vexilla Regis* by David Jones?) In the north there had for centuries been a dearth of devotional poetry of any grip or dazzle—until recent years when the natural eloquence of George Mackay Brown, at home in the element, was joined by Tom Leonard's 'Good Thief' and Alastair Mackie's 'Pieta'. So from the nineteen-fifties and again in the last years of her life, a woman poet of Scotland shows that various streams of religious lyric once running strong in these islands can still break out in the parched north.

A third mode of lyric was very much in her mind when she settled in Greenwich in 1939, living by her pen or from

38

casual work in very humble circumstances indeed. This was a new poetry for Scotland that used the land itself as ground for poetic creativity—its topography and history, its legend and its tongues. Of the languages that belong to Scotland or had left their mark on it she drew on almost all. There was a programme of study. She read on from Anglo-Saxon and Old Norse of her university years through the earlier ages of Scotland's history, conscious of the Nordic heritage as well as the Celtic. Her prize poem of 1935 in Cambridge, 'The Vikings', had discovered in the Battle of Largs, 1263, a conflict of Nord and Celt that she discerned within her own mind and personality. Taking this further, she hit on the theme of the *gaul gael,* the apostate gone back from Celtic Christendom to the old gods of the north, from Christ to Odin: *For such a one as Torquil Mor, Odin will come in his great ship Skidbladnir, to claim his soul—come on the Eve of St Mark, for on that night souls due to die within the year are at risk and can be glimpsed by the watcher.* This last we know from Keats' poem of the same title—the link of the new poem with old is overt. Olive Fraser's poem 'The Eve of St Mark' is unfinished, as was its forebear. This piece of dark enchantment carries Keats' theme, devised afresh, into a territory unfrequented by southern poetry. It is a new blend of imagining.

On the Celtic side Olive Fraser was reading Adamnan's *Life of Columba, Carmina Gadelica* and early lyrics of Ireland. She was not herself a Gaelic speaker, but was learning Gaelic now, as grammatical jottings among her papers show. A child of Nairn, her own speech was 'highland English' but she had a masterly command of Scots, both the speech of the north-east (within earshot for her in school and college days) and the language of earlier Scots poetry. Her lyrics in Scots of 1951 show a deft use of early forms, bird-debate of lowland thrush versus highland eagle or, in 'All Sawles' Eve', a *chanson d'aventure* ('I went out on a named day and perceived a wonder.') She can also flyte in Scots and deliver an axe-blow at the end—as in 'Requiem for Dives'. She can modulate from Scots into English or *vice versa* with telling effect and can pun on a Scots sense of a word against the English one, as in 'ditty'/song, 'dittay'/in Scots law an indictment, or heavy charge laid on one, or undertaken. ('V.E. Day 1945')

But it was her love for the land itself, the high lands and wild peaks of Scotland that led her to ponder the placenames of the

39

north as they recorded man's sense of belonging—to this burn, that hillside, with peak or mountain range his fellow from morning till night, a landscape of his mind: say Buachaille Eite—the shepherd of Etive, guardian of the smaller summits around him, or the Mither Tap of the peaks of Bennachie. In this mode of poem, 'Harpsong for Alban' or 'The Eagle to his Children'—a placename is a landmark for a thought, a series of placenames unrolls a sequence of poetic meaning. It may have a particular association for the poet herself or it may, by indicating a territory of her forebears, her family or clan, involve the poet's own innermost concern. Her Gaelic spelling, often antiquated or mistaken, is amended in the notes, pp.205–10.

Placenames in sequence can not only bring the colour and character of each peak or island to mind, they also scan the great region visible to the human eye from a favourable vantage-point. The outstanding poem here is 'To Night'. It is cosmic in scope. The word 'house' releases a vast range of significances: on earth a home for men or wild creatures, a holy place, a temple, a college; in astral terms a division of the skies, a place of zodiac sign or planet—and in heavenly dimensions one of the mansions of God. The House of Night is raised by incantation, by subtle iteration of key-words 'mountains' and 'thee', as by chime of rhyme and refrain. The wild hare and all homing birds *belong,* as do the mountain peaks and islands named. Man is incomer—with an exile's longing for home or the ardent desire of the early Celtic religious to seek sanctity in the wilderness. These two contrary impulses are reconciled in the poet's joy.

Yet another kind of poetry emerged in the fifties as Olive Fraser meditated on the nature of poetry itself and on the poet's calling, which she saw as a vocation and also as a sentence to poverty. A sequence of lyrics entitled 'The Poet' was ready by 1954. Of the scope of the poet's calling in time and in space she had no doubt. 'The Poet (I)' is dated 1949 but was probably drafted in 1940, when she was a Wren in a Scots naval base at Rosyth, and the 'dear land' in danger was both Scotland and 'the visionary land' of poesie, as defended centuries earlier by Sir Philip Sidney. Scotland she spans in space from Dunedin (Edinburgh) in the east to Duntulm in the west, an ancient fortress of the MacDonalds, her kin. The visionary land she spans in time from the poet in uniform writing now back to classical antiquity, to Thebes, where the all conquering

Alexander spared the house that had been Pindar's. At mid-vista, in seventeenth-century London, stands John Milton, pinning a sonnet on his door 'When the Assault was intended to the city'. By power of placename, through heritage of poetry and of native land, she says it in eight lines: 'The Visionary Land'/'The Poet (I)'.

In 1954 she wrote a manifesto under the same title, 'The Poet', but signed 'Poeta', perhaps because the Latin word embraced the woman writer in her. Speaking memorably both of poet as inspired and as sentenced to poverty, it was written in hope of reaching print as a riposte to an article in *The Sunday Times* (March 5th) by Felix Barker, entitled 'Genius Unknown: Report on Youth'. He had asserted that the nineteen fifties were much harder for young poets than the nineteen thirties had been. She disagreed.

. . . In the past 20 years I have won 22 literary prizes and 2 gold medals and I have managed to publish 7 small poems and a short story. People who do not write might wonder why or how I go on. Well, wait till I find the New Testament, which is somewhere in this clutter.

See, in the Gospel of St John, where Jesus says to the Twelve, 'Will you also go away?' and St Peter answers 'Lord, to whom shall we go? Thou hast the words of eternal life.'

That's it. It is not possible to turn away. The very thought of never experiencing again that strange visitation of a power unknown which precedes the writing of poetry is something to make one willing to accept all things. Not that I have ever liked being hungry or poor. But if that's the way it has got to be, I would rather have it that way than not at all . . .

Hunger, sickness, loneliness, uncertainty and frustration are easier things to bear when one is older. They may even, if you can bear them long enough, be mysteriously valuable. But you will never write what you might have written, because you will no longer be the same person. That person, whom nature sent into the world with an equipment she devised for the first time and which she will never repeat anywhere, is dead. You may if you have the singular desire to write which makes all distresses ghosts, write far better than if you had never known these distresses, but the first poet will have to die first . . .

I would not like to bet on something so rare and miraculous as the rising of the phoenix because I think that many true poets have died from discouragement for whom no phoenix has ever risen . . .

The joy at her all too late transformation into health that she expresses in the letters to Elma Mennie is found transmuted into poetry in 'Prayer to a Tree'. 'The withered husk that clings to you', herself before treatment, seeks betterment from contact with the freshly-growing graceful tree. This poem has no date attached. Perhaps written before in longing, or afterwards in grateful poetic 'recollection', it reveals a secret source of the poet's strength. 'Fill me anew like Hellespont . . .' The place-name is immediately understandable, for Hellespont is 'the journeying sea' of Leander swimming to his Hero and it is 'the icy current and compulsive course' of the lines from Othello, figuring the huge vitality of the universe. But it is more. Close by Hellespont (and therefore in the old sense 'resembling it', as 'the nearest thing to it') grew the sympathetic trees, sprung from the spot where fell in battle the first victim of the Trojan War, the beloved of Laodamia. As these trees grew tall enough to glimpse with their tops the dreadful sight of Troy, these tops withered and shrivelled . . . but were constantly renewed. This wisdom of antique fable belongs to the main heritage of English poetry for Wordsworth drew on it for his poem 'Laodamia'. Olive Fraser had within her not only the inherited wealth of poetry but also the creature-wisdom to know where to go for healing—counter-magic for shrivelling disease as for deadly injury by war. And she had the talent thereafter to transmit to us that solace.

The early poetry needs to be described as an achievement of twenty years writing even though, in a sense, it never happened since poet and her whole range of poetry never encountered the eye, ear and mind of the general public of the time. It is there as a living process, preserved, as it were, in amber. On the other hand the poetry Olive Fraser wrote from the moment of even partial restoration to health when lyrics flowed abundantly from her pen, is accessible to us, contemporary if strange. She writes in old-style poet's grammar and her thought is under discipline of stanza and rhyme. Her argument strides with swingeing power through a whole poem, sometimes in one sentence. But everywhere she shows 'the sense of musical delight' so seldom heard today.

Now a choice has been possible from some three hundred lyrics, the whole life-span of writing. Not only is the whole range of earlier poetry revealed but for the older poet we see that great new highways have opened. 'The suffering has been mysteriously valuable'. There are verses of hate, discord and despair but far more of remembrance and reconciliation, of past suffering become solace, of the search for love that belongs to the human heart and also to the heavenly kingdom.

I claim for this poet, who belongs to the great old tradition of poetry, the classic poetic virtues: her poetry gives 'instruction' and 'delight'. It gives instruction by widening our consciousness and understanding of the order of nature in all creation. Her friends used to refer to 'the kind of thing that Olive knows': that Herb Trinity is heartsease, remembrance and is also 'three faces under a hood' of covert activity ('The Corner Shop'). That the burnet leaf and the wild plantain are vulnerary herbs, remedy for the wounded and the plaintain is also a love-charm and a revealer of lies ('Tell the wild plantain'). That Virgo in the heavens is the zodiac sign and also The Blessed Virgin, intercessor, 'the pleading star', while 'the innate word of mosses' recalls that dendrites, the mosslike, treelike formations in stone were regarded as 'signatures' of God marking the work of his hand traceable throughout creation.

> The pleading star, the innate word of mosses
> O, the unchanging gold.
>
> ('A Shelf of Books')

These two together betoken the sister truths of religion and science, the thought of man leaving its mark on the universe. Olive Fraser's poems of Scotland show 'the dear land' in universal terms, where man, bird, beast, fish, plant and stone of the mountains are in place in the order of nature, and the intricately ordered poem celebrates that harmony. But instruction is there also in the sense of moral excellence in comment, reverent or irreverent, on human behaviour.

But 'delight' is there too, in the old sense of sudden recognition of an identity unperceived before, in, for example, root and branches of a word. I know of no other poet in modern times who can so rouse

43

the reverberations of meaning within a word, meaning perhaps dormant within its root-sense, or, having blossomed earlier, now rare or especial in application. Another primary source of delight is in the poetic image emerging as resolution of a psychological crisis, for which I cite 'Hellespont' which I spoke of earlier. In 'A Nocturnal to Poetry', 'evening' is the coming-on of eve, an evening spent often in a festive manner; it is also a balancing-out and a comparing. A galaxy, in the poem of the night-train, is, in the strict dictionary sense, 'a luminous band or track . . . consisting of innumerable points of light'. In 'The Fire of Apple Wood' 'gorgeous' can be a mere epithet of approbation, but it can still denote splendour of colour. Indeed, 'the gorgeous north' in a context of snow holds us as by an apparent paradox. But the line that is to follow

> The north falls with his green light round
> My shaking life . . .

expounds all. The colour-show that belongs to the north, suffused with green, is the Aurora Borealis. 'Shaking' belongs to the whole poem as well as to its immediate noun. In Olive Fraser's later writing there is, in many poems, a key word. With it a word-hoard is unlocked, revealing unexpected meanings and associations, each perfectly applied. And these bring within hearing the undersong or subtext of the poetry.

Olive Fraser had a word for this magic, 'exact felicity'. She uses it in 'To an Unknown Ancestor, Maybe'. The phrase exemplifies what it defines. Felicity is happiness but also signifies poetic mastery, the achievement of the happy phrase, the felicitous expression, the word of overall relevance that belongs to the poem as a whole as well as performing its immediate task, a strikingly pertinent expression. 'Exact' is consummate, finished, perfect, perfectly corresponding. But it is also at its root 'arising from the performance'. Exact felicity is not only the achievement of the perfect term in a poem but the happiness arisen from that achievement. Olive Fraser knew both.

Helena Shire

*Student Days*
*Nairn, Aberdeen, Cambridge*
*1928–1936*

# A Horse Drinking

A boy shall hold his cup
  To the white horse riding by,
Gold eyes and laughing lips
  Of the red mulberry.

The white mane stoops to drink
  Child's eyes and dark are strained
Gold eyes and dark to the brink
  Till all the cup is drained.

Down slips the peerless face
  The white wave into the red.
Breathless, tiptoe, above
  A boy's enchanted head.

Dark eyes below the brink
  Gold eyes above
Love deep down in the cup
  And over, Love.

1929

# Biviers
## in the foothills of the French Alps

Tempests of light and tides of day,
I used to think in Biviers,
Made up man's life and boundless seas
Of mighty immortalities.

When I shall never see again
Snows, cirques, cascades, rain,
Nor watch the sun's eye turning grey
From the hill road at Biviers,

O let the Belledonne's snowy crest
Still bow in beauty on my breast.
Let the wild hawk of Chartreuse climb
Over my head at sleeping-time;

And I shall lie content all day
With that great life at Biviers,
Where the crag's tumult seemed to me
Overtures of eternity.

1929

## Christopher steals a road-mender's lantern

Christopher steals a road-mender's lantern
    At the crossing-gates to Nod.
'O the little red lamp is beauty
    And I am God.

'I walk along the road-ways
    Little head ever so high,
Where the road-makers leave their lamps to light
    The spirit-people by.

'I walk along the highways
    No squeak of the mouse or the mole—
This beauty it must be all my own
    It strikes so near my soul.

48

'Soft, I take up my lantern
    Quick, quick, I steal away.
I will hug my beauty all night long
    For it goes at the day.'

February 1930


## Grey Goose Walking

There are two little lanes and a white bird-cherry
And Grey Goose Water right at the end,
And Grey Goose walking and walking merry
At market morning with twopence to spend;

Two goose pennies and a goose-feather farthing
To buy gold butter at Doubleduck Fair,
And Grey Goose walking and walking merry
With the little brown rabbit and the little dun hare.

The hill face smiles and the hill winds listen,
And proud they walk when the sheep look down,
And high they are walking and walking merry
With the two goose pennies to Doubleduck town.

O they lift little feet and they step so straightly
When Hay Wagon Horse comes over the hill,
And high they are walking and walking merry
With the goose-feather farthing at Doubleduck mill.

There are two little lanes and a white bird-cherry
And Grey Goose Water right away there,
And Grey Goose walking and walking merry
With the little brown rabbit and the little dun hare.

Tomintoul (Easter) 1930

## To a Parent

Hadst thou thought once on me, thy love less mean
I should have walked with rarer stars today
But thou didst get me in a grove unseen
And kept me hid out of the common way
And I fast knew that I should ne'er have been
And was thy burden and thy life's decay.

And to this hour I shrink and ne'er answer
The call of the engrossing world to go
Outward to haste to play as tho' I were
The black sign that thy frighted heart did know,
A creature of no country, and the heir
Of joys that climbed not, but sought depths below

The happy merry things of life and left
Me but a near-ghost, thy love still a theft.

26th June 1930

## Sing, o bird, for love is dead

Sing, o bird, for love is dead
He who kept thy soul awake
Singing for his lovely sake
Lies with cypress round his head.
Sing, o bird, for love is dead.

Smile, o maid, and take delight,
At thy silver casement more
Love shall ply his descants o'er
Never, tho' the moon shine bright.
Smile, o maid, and take delight.

Joy, o heart, and go thy way.
All love's royal tales and false
Broken are, with madrigals
That did thee of old bewray.
Joy, o heart, and go thy way.

Stars shall be less bright and rare,
Yet this world, now love is dead,
Scarce so dark as souls he fled,
But, my soul, consider there,
Stars shall be less bright and rare.

1931

## Sequence from 'Fugue of Morning'

*quo fugit venator, per silvam, per vitam?*

### I.

The snow of all the Appenine is gone
    Down to the chasms of the summer. Lie
The old range of the Alps like to a stone
    Which nature framed of the light porphyry.
Now wakes the hare. Now the mergansers fly
    Like ghosts around the mountain tops. The swan
And the wild dotterel of the hills all lie
    Scattered in their dark sleeping-holes upon
The lonely cliffs until silence and sleep are done.

## 2.

O little speechless ones what do they know
    In the great night when all the stars are still?
What thinks the osprey, what the stone curlew
    In these deep hours, and does the lone whimbrel
Utter his faint pipe once upon the hill
    For very fear and then for fear again
Grow hushed as death, nestles each trembling quill
    Close in the heather? Does the dipper's strain
On the wild torrent wake his fearful sense again?


## 3.

Come is the dawn, and like a spirit shout
    The clamorous kennel up the hunting morn.
Lo! the falcons of the sky leap out, out, out,
    Straight wing, clear eye, illimitably borne
Through the late stars, the circumstance forlorn
    Of the wide air. Against their grey breasts fly
The flying dark. Trembles the happy horn
    Up through the winds, and speeds the daylight nigh
The shipping of the East, the fast sails of the sky.


## 4.

The year is up. Now is Orion come
    With hunting to the great house of the Spring . . .

 . . . .

19.

A light there is, the fields of earth adorning.
    The crying in the darkness is half told.
Rises up like a bird the great high morning
    Sets on the grey hills top the marvellous gold
Saying with joy, 'This world is never old.'
    Look out, and when Time's battlements are gone
The unincarnate terraces unfold
    Of all the mountains laughing to the sun
In the eternal world of the eternal One.


20.

So hunter, run the merry horn along
    The haunted floors of forests, hear thy horse
Most fiercely beat that ancient running song
    Which Charlemain evoked from the old course
Of the Pyrénez when his darling force
    His cavalcades over the rocks of Spain
Poured their black warsong and the horn's remorse
    Of the great Roland struck that lonely plain
—Roland and thou shall ride to Roncevalles again.


1931


## Apple land and fallow gray

Apple land and fallow gray
And fall of mist at holyday . . .
Eaves and sheaves and crowded leaves
And God you bless at holyday.
When I am tired of hills and ways
Long, long yet in the afterdays,
And mirth and masques and orchards deep

And market ale and country sleep
And steadfast children gravely brown
And clocks about an old Basque town—
When I am tired of the apple-prime
Blown like a happy harvest-time
In the rich ruin of wrecked hay
A tumbled passion of granary;
I will go down with lonely face
Old landscapes to the loneliest place
Remembering how dawn could be
The vesper of our company
And whose wit crept to bed at four
To rise at nine with further store,
And who had curls, and who gold hair
And who could play a pixy air
And all slept deep and all could be
A charming silent company.

+ (because Jean is annoyed)

Jean

When softly steps the forest fawn
Through the pale sonatas of the dawn
There is one bullies me to make
An end of sleep for coffee's sake.
There is one bends her able mind
To torturing poor human kind.
There is one lends no ear to sorrow . . .
And I shall *not* get up tomorrow.

New Pitsligo 1931

# The Vikings

*King Hako's navy met on St Laurence Wake in 1263 at Ronaldsvo*
*under the leadership of his great ship Brimvald.*

I saw the dead upon St Laurence Wake
    Sailing in beautiful Brimvald. They were young,
Younger than death and life, with a sweet tongue
    I have heard in my blood before,
Dreaming it was the wild gannets that make
    Their comment upon Sulna-stapa shore.
I cried upon the dead, 'Why is your face
    So beautiful in the regretless place?

'Surely among the dead there is no will
    For dragon-necks of gold and for straight sails,
And Brimvald with the silver bitterns' tails
    Is quiet under dark skerries now.'
'O we are loved among the living still,
    We are forgiven among the dead. We plough
In the old narrows of the spirit. We
    Have woven our wealth into your mystery.'

And I remembered words that I had heard
    And never heard. And vessels that I knew
And thought were visions. The mute swans that flew
    Over grey islands were like these
And yet were nothing. Once at Herlesferd
    I saw a ship whose path on the green seas
Made joy to brindled sea-birds, and my breath
    Was dangerous and scant, bitter like death.

'O if you died upon St Laurence Wake
    Why are you beautiful and young,' I cried
'Like dreams of you I saw on a great tide
    Lovelier and more young than I?
Even when I heard the wild white eagles take
    Over the earth with their cruel minstrelsy
You were more light than I have ever been.'
    They said 'We are your Soul that you have seen.'

1935


## A Nocturnal to Poetry

Let us lie still and let the world dispense
All rest and beauty to our sense.
Neither aconite nor satyrian do blow
Awhile upon the spring,
So we will go
Into a winter or an evening.

Rivers dry up and care not, and so we
Will be dried up as carelessly,
Nor any fountain will we echo for long
Nor any other voice,
But when all song
Is silent through the air, ours will rejoice.

And since all heavenly birds all music say,
Unlike this heart, at break of day,
Nor pray cold stars to light their litanies by,
But fall in slumber deep,
We too comply.
We have stayed out of bed and now must sleep.

Cambridge 1936

56

## Envoi to Poetry

My lovely visitor, thou must go
Unto Proserpina's dark gate and say
That I have sent at last my soul away
For she, poor migrant one doth know
That the wild nightingale will never sing
In hell that should have had so fair a spring.

There thou must say thou found'st in me
A cheerless hostel to my holy guest
And where thou should'st have seen so great a feast
Thou only hadst great poverty.
Then run thee to Proserpina my light
And leave me to my everlasting night.

1936

*War and After War*
*1940–1949*

## To The Last Generation

*(Lines Written in the Naval Base, Aberdeen)*

In the years to come
When thou dost bolt the door
Of the useless house
Think what went before.

For thy navies new
The oak grove springs wild
But what blest field will know
The feet of thy child?

October 1940

## The Sleeper

*(from a quiet night-watch on Liverpool docks)*

All the holy sea sleeps here
In this quiet sleeper's ear.
The winds for his great vessel, his Andromache
Dwell in this blood's profundity.
O enchanted west,
O thou huge east that settest never in this breast,
You royal heads and oceans lone
Whose dawns yet shine in this entrancèd bone,
And the inbearing tide,
That with his brain some music dost divide,
Currents in azure straits that rise,
And the south and the north skies,

And planets, stars that never part
But make your zodiac this heart—
Ye never silent, silence keep
In this dim room, in this unstirring sleep.

1941


## To Poetry

*(Written in St Francis Hospital, East Dulwich)*

Follow, my ghost, unto the hills of gold
Faithful, unfearing, tho' thy beauty die
Til the lit boughs of heaven shine in our fold
Our swans come home out of the western sky.

Let us be tried, married in mystery
Each unto each, by dearth, by bitter fear.
Let us be tried, but do thou part from me
Never in heaven or earth, my sword-bearer.

? 1941


## Pastoral

All my little red cocks run
Home to roost at set of sun.
All my pretty pullets dream.
No one speaks but Meadow Stream.
Meadow Stream says over and over
'O my milfoils! O my clover!

Sleep, sleep, grey rat, sleep
In my bank safe and deep.
Sleep, sleep, water hen,
On your nine brown eggs in my glen.
All my nenuphars and mints
Sleep softly in the moon's tints.
Sleep, my little silver trout,
In my bed 'til night is out.'

?Nairn 1942

## The Pilgrim

I have no heart to give thee, for I
Am only groundmists and a thing of wind,
And the stone echoes under bridges and the kind
Lights of high farms, the weary watchdog's cry.

I have no desire for thy dreams, for my own
Are no dreams, but realities which are
The blind man's sight, the sick man's heavenly star
Fire of the homeless, to no other known.

1943

## On a Distant Prospect of Girton College

Here the snow beats her flowers of fate
On my soul's gate.

Here the redbreast weeps again
For the world of men.

Here the child cries, cries wild,
Ever for the lost child.

Here the maiden lays her down
Her shroud her wedding gown.

Here does heavenly Plato snore,
A cypher, no more.

Here Herodotus goes by
At many knots, silently.

Here sits Dante in the dim
With Freud watching him.

Here does blessed Mozart seem
Alas, a sensual dream.

Here I could curse the hearts that shred
The great roses of the dead.

Here does holy innocence crave
A convent or a grave.

Here does Love lose his wings
Where women are female things.

Here is virginity thought to be
A state of the flesh only.

Here, my blood, muffle thy drum
Lest the hangman come.

Here, my muse, as we had died,
Sleep or be crucified.

Here's not thy Parnassus bright
But Hecla's icy light

O here do never, never come
Pure spring, perfect autumn.

1943

# The Home Fleet

Across my lawn, upon the dawn
The broad-keeled cabbages set sail,
A fleet complete with hearts as sweet
As ever yet for England beat,
The borekail and the kail.

Lo, when my lurching galleons ride
Upon the north wind side by side
Tho' 'Guns and butter' Hitler said
'Guns and cabbages' wakes the dead,
A creaking shanty on the air.
The morning thrush wakes up to stare.

Neath the late stars with masts and spars
That yet will fill my pickle jars
'Express' and 'Harbinger' lean and mutter,
'More Heinkels lying about the gutter
In most unholy disrepair!
Whoever can have put them there?'
And 'Guns and cabbages' wakes the deaf,
'Cabbages for the R.A.F.!'

When to their Plate (no lesser there
Than 'Ajax' or bright 'Exeter'!)
My cabbages' hearts are vanished all
And I, their earthy admiral
Stay useless here, some voice will rise
From these poor stumps of argosies
Till 'Guns and cabbages' still I hear
Victorious upon the year.

1943

# V.E. Day 1945

Thrang, thrang's the fowk in the wide city
But my luve's nae there.
My luve is won awa frae ilka ditty,
He daunces at nae fair.

O harp, ye harpers, while I climb upward at even
By my auld wearie stair.
The sun bends doon, the laverock comes hame frae
heaven,
But my luve nae mair.

Before 1951


## Victory Ode

Dear land, no music suits this glorious day
Like thy own music. Thames and Tyne rejoice,
Grey patient London and proud Coventry,
All cities have a voice.
Hark to the merry Atlantic shout, the lay
Of the cold Pentland; hear the Channel's glee.
Thy thousand sweet embattled hamlets say
An ode more dear than mine. Yet I would call
Great names and comrades to thy festival.

I call the dead first; martyrs, prisoners.
I call the blood of Breendonck from its ease,
But find that it has grown on the earth a sun
And lights men's destinies.
Yet ne'er was such a sunrise. Shed your tears
Who walk beneath this lustre. This— begun
In dungeons, graves, must blaze on all the years.
Instruct your judgments, heirs. Or, perishing, say
'Vain was their murdered blood, vain victory.'

O world, I have no mystery nor art
To praise thy phalanxes. In Sicily,
The desert, Vistula, or in the Rhine
Or in the dangerous sea
Lies many a friend. Give me yet Orpheus' heart
To pierce the night, and lead your loves to shine
In their old place. Lo! on a word they start
Or on a vision, and all their glories burn
Among the living still, through earth, through urn.

I never knew in the world my faithful love
(A cobbled port, an ancient stony crown,)
So rare as now. Think in thy silent mind
And put thy true love down
And thank thy fellow men and God above
She sits in light and freedom. Let no blind
And envious enemy disturb her grove
Or our loved isle. And may this peace be great
Tho' one dear head lacks our triumvirate.

## In Memory of one who loved me

My dear light lies a land away
Underneath in hollow
Precious darkness. Let her stay.
O let no word of mine or vision follow
To bring her to the world today.

We had on earth for envious love
No peace, respite never.
Now she goes with the saints above
And I, left yet alive, our loves now sever,
Lying in the wild apple grove.

Berkshire 1945


## The Empty House

The sun is set. The grey night grows
From my heart like a rose
Petal on petal, finds each room
And builds it fast within the gloom.
No flower did show nor the wild linnet call
Upon thy funeral.
This dark flower then I gave
To be, not mark, thy second grave.

Thick does it thrive on board and floor
And the mocking door
Where thou com'st not. O death—night—laugh
That I made but a cenotaph
For her. Retire. It is indeed a tomb.
Here since she never will come
It is I who perish by
Some clock striking eternity.

1946

68

# Upon an Irish Terrier, Quip.

### I

Persephone, look from thy darkened gate
And stay o'er Styx the ever-during sleet,
For by that bank doth my Quipinus wait
Who will not cross save at his mistress' feet.

### II

Still by the Styx doth my Quipinus err
And still maraud among the Stygian teal,
A curse to Charon, crippled, who can ne'er
Catch him, nor, toothless, whistle him to heel.

### III

The wild stars look in the dark brakes, Quipinus.
No star doth show me now thy small head,
My runner, the sweet-throated, my little Quipinus
Who hunts with the dead.

### IV

In this small tomb all faultless love doth end:
My dog, Quipinus, and my dearest friend.

### V

O Time, the memory of Quipinus save
That 'Friend' may in the world a meaning have.

1946

## The King's Student

All men do sleep in night and darkness dead
Save thee, Callimachus, reading in bed.
Thy windy candle lights a page, a part,
But an old hoary lantern lights thy heart.

Aberdeen 1946

## To a ship

When I am dead, when all my powers are death,
　　Lovely Skidbladnir, strike for me
One song, one breath,
Ye divine waves of Scapa, let there be
But one wave 'neath her foot that glorieth
　　That I may dream upon the peerless sea.

1946

## On a neglected Vocation

O my dark ghost, who knowest thy sole fountain
Turn to the secret water. Thou
Too long dost labour on a desperate mountain
Too long amid the world dost bow
Too long thy light my life denieth
Tho' the great air is sweet and thee
Crown'd with thy dreams, like the wild swan that
　　　　　　　　　　　　　　　flieth
Back to her own sea.

1946

## On a stoned and dying Cygnet

O king, dream not upon the fabulous air
And, dreaming, beat, and beating, wounded wake.
I have a passion that my heart must bear
And thou hast one that thine will break.

I weep for thee on thy last pool's last brink,
The royal ruin'd head, bewrayèd wing,
But in thy death 'tis of my kin I think
With horror, grief past uttering.

Bedford 1946


## On the Departure of the Osprey
## from Loch an Eilean

*(Ospreys mate for life. The female was shot by a 'sportsman',
and the male returned for seven years to the eyrie.)*

All that my heart loved and long held in dream
Sacred above all other earth, dark stream,
Dark ancient mountain, bowing on the day,
With thy she-eagle slain, thyself did'st slay.

Long for old joy such havoc, grief did reign,
Thou wert no home unto my heart again,
Poor rock, his home, all his poor hope, who sate
Seven years, seven tempests, by his murdered mate.

O cradle of our beauty, still at last,
In peace farewell, farewell for ever past,
Never to light again our loves in dream,
Thou ancient mountain, thou dark, ancient stream.

? 1946

71

## The Unfading Thing

In our old days and quiet grove
When our true sun did shine
One cup of water from thy hand, my love
Was worth the world of wine.

Long thou dost lie the world outwith
Both wine and water done,
Yet in my songs there still, still lingereth
The last light of our sun.

23rd May 1947


## Tell the wild plantain

Tell the wild plantain
Growing on the mountain.
Tell the burnet leaf
But not thy dear love.

Thy faith the fierce hover
Will keep forever.
The little roe will save
Not thy dear love.

All snows that thrive
All rivers that strive
All evils, long survive
Thy dear love.

1947

## Summer Dusk 1947

Now the trout leaps where none may see
God's holy will within the wasting rings,
Now does the great house of eternity
Rise from all country roads and common things
Upon the earth. The shrew-mouse creeps
Unto that door. The little moorhen sleeps.

All sleep, but their lover who must
In silence lean and dream upon his art,
Hearing until the world fall to dust
Only the hourbook of the wild bird's heart
The landrail at her mysteries
For angels' ears that lean by shoreless seas.

1947

## In a City Street

I had forgot, my love, that thou wert dead
And happily, happily said 'I must go home.'
And suddenly the stars strayed, sudden fled
Unto the towers like terrified birds, the foam
Of monstrous oceans broke over my head.
I had forgot, my love, that thou wert dead.

1947

# The Mountain Bird—The Dipper

(On the children of Nairn killed in Exmouth
and in Prince of Wales.)

O mountain bird, sing to the stream
And let thy white breast tremble on the stones
And let the wild stream bear thy song away
Unto the sea and to the silent bones
Of David, Diarmid, Lesley, Antony,

All those who loved this little stream
All those who played beside this quiet hill
All those who saw in dreams this holy glen
All of Fearna's friends who never will
See their dear home or their wild bird again.

Oxford 1947


# After War (I)

Still do I trust to Thy divinity
And to no sign, when all my light is fled.
Thou Saviour of the living and the dead,
Still doth Thy servant list, as I
Blessèd, had heard Thy voice at Caesarea Philippi.

After great war, out of the dreadful grave
Of truth, dumb to myself, Thou canst me read.
When I walk 'twixt the living and the dead,
Thou canst alone my darkness save,
Immanuel, who call Thy name, no other angel have.

Where Thou did'st bend amid the deadly night
Thro' death, thro' flames, a branch of beauty spread.
Then, as not now, the living and the dead
Were one fast fort in me, Thy Light
Beyond the murdered ships, beyond the burning world, our
might.

I have a winter only Thou dost see
And pitiest, when all my light is fled,
For now the living, the forgotten dead
Rise up and strive again in me,
And all things ashes are, deserts, monstrous futility.

All the bewrayèd blood of earth doth cry
About my dreams, like weary bondslaves led,
The wanton living, and the wasted dead,
Genius torn from her sacred sky,
And innocence perished in stews, and dreams perished for aye.

Here doth the violence of the mad world come
Nightly to threaten by my sleepless bed,
Until I think the living are the dead
Stinking in tombs. It is the dead who roam
Beauteous as stars, beloved like truth, spirits from towers of
foam.

Then in this waste where famine, penury
Make me at last to think Thy glory fled,
O shine betwixt the living and the dead
Search in these snows. O succour me,
Who else in night perish, but never in the world find Thee.

1947–8

## After War (II)

Thou no more dost seek the ghost
Beauteous, beckoning from the past,
But dwell'st by thy great sun, thy Host
Who crowns thy blood at last
Beyond war, beyond the word,
Beyond the music of the mid-sea bird.

Never riot turns thee now
From thine own. Thy spirit caught
Of old by many a shining prow
Of glory, knows it naught,
But knows all motion and all strife
Of men and ages a disguise of life.

Thou hast died to know this hour
Somewhat. Bless thy death and bless
Relinquished love, the tyrant's power,
The liar's heart, duress,
The darkening sight, all wounds that gave
Thee, still alive, the freedom of the grave.

Take thy freedom, then and go—
Whither? Never do I dream
What world can receive this snow
What heart this hurtless stream,
Since in the world the dead man's bone
Loud cries o'er all, saving the dead alone.

? 1947

## November Cockcrow

I saw my love in an old ghostly town
In mountains. Her sick voice was harsh and hoar
As I did hear it a long age before
In pathless winter. Then the winds blew down.
The cocks crowed, and I woke and wept to know
That thou, dust of the grave, my dear, thou less
Than all things, shelterest still, poor nothingness,
Still to my heart in pain or light must go.
O Chanticleer, reach thou and cry again
And cry her custom to the inveterate world.
Bid forth the winter lanterns, hasting feet,
And the grey dogs. O cry up all amain.
Thou hast no art to affright one phantom curled
Nor the crowds fasten, where my life doth beat.

Oxford 1948


## Within this little testament

Within this little testament
A pretty kingdom is to rent.
Search in those pages 'til ye see
At last your lost herb trinity—
And all the lesser herbs that make
Strength and delight for Christ his sake.
Read in these verses 'til ye find
The holy office of the mind
Where pain keeps out, the senses rest
As calm as thrushes on their nest.
There the sick heart still finds a place
Among the glades, byroads of grace,
Within this dog-eared testament
Where such a kingdom is to rent.

1948

# In a Glen Garden (After War)

*Abdolonymus was a gardener, and yet by Alexander for his virtues made King of Syria. (Burton's* Anatomy of Melancholy.*)*

Afar in the bright sun
The furious world doth run,
But here a tree doth stay me
Lest the world slay me.

Nothing clearly I see
My life fallen from me,
But the starling searcheth the plot
As death were not.

The sunlight sleepeth here
And the William pear,
Never to war growing
Nought on earth knowing.

Were all these garden things,
Their silences, the bastionings
Of Alexander's power
In their unnoticed hour?

I think his victories
Were but tranquillities.
I have seen death so oft
Where he hath slumbered soft.

I have seen Sirius fly
It seemed, the ruined sky,
And the babe in gobbets fall
By the burning wall.

And the thunder that smote the roof
Was never Bucephalus' hoof,
But the cloven night that came
Calling the souls in flame,

Yet the ship that perished in stars
Was thy ship, O Mars,
In my sense still to ride
As once on Mersey tide.

I cannot rest again
For the work my life did then,
My art deep buried beneath
The roaring moon of death.

My mind half-wedded is
To war as with a kiss,
But my forefathers rise
In holier mysteries.

An old man's ghost leaneth
By my young hands. Wind gleaneth
Nor telleth here our story
Piteous since mine is hoary.

Yet of the tree's answer
My heart no word doth hear,
Tho' in old time it would
Read in the secret wood.

Do thou, O William pear
Sweeten the silent air
'Til to the sharded house
Comes Abdolonymus.

1949

# In a Hill Garden

*(Written after service in the R.N. Base, Liverpool.)*

Thee, thou old Syrian man, we never knew,
But know among the hills the sweet air yet
In this high garden. The grey violet,
Grey scabious dwell. Wind-loving feverfew
Bows at the door, thy country ghost to us
Welcome, old king, old Abdolonymus.

1949


# The Tree

Who art thou, O tree?
Once a bird sang in me,
Once the bright moon shone silently
On the blackbird in me.
O happy tree!

Yea, God builded me
From the abyss tenderly,
Taught my wild singer his glee,
The woods rang with me.
Happy tree!

Nay, men came for me,
Drave my poor bird from me,
Brake his nest utterly.
No music ever for me.
Alas, slain tree!

Nay, God lifted me
From the stars so kindly
Bended in blood under me.
O where was this, dark tree?
Mount Calvary.

Oxford 1949

*Greenwich*
*1949–1954*

# A cold night on Croome's Hill in London

Cold is the autumn evening
Only one bird doth sing,
And one tree holds his branches
For the last singing thing.
One sinner goes unsigned.
Unfed, one infant freezes.
The leaves drift down blood-red
Beside the feet of Jesus.

1949

# Lo, tho' I show thee

Lo, tho' I show thee
The wild pink's scent
The road of the wild snowgoose
The song of the sea-bent,
My friend, this is the martyr's way
The way that Jesus went.

Shut thou the door. Turn
Tho' angels thee invite,
Out of the ice, taunts, prisons,
Safe to the red firelight,
Unless, maybe, thy stars are such
As will outlast the night.

1949

## The Visionary Land—The Poet I

Let the wind pay the ditty
Thy drink be winter's rain.
Keep for thy old age thy pity
So my dear land remain.

Not thee, Dunedin hoary
Not Duntulm's kingly shore
But thyself, Thebes, Thebes thou glory
Writ on an old door.

1949


## On an old woman

No beauty in the world or in the sky
Repays thine absence. But Andrea dead,
Unto the orphan the ungrudged bread,
The fire, the book, the heavenly charity,
Shelter of my wan childhood, thy old heart
Quenched in the grave, still lights my living art.

1949

## Long do the stone and echoing tree

Long do the stone and echoing tree
Speak in the world after the voice is dead.
Tho' silently
The winter thrush, singing aloof
By the hoar drop, at last is fled
She leaves her music in the forest roof.

O winter land and O wan time
By thee I live, so keep my shades aright.
Strive not; nor climb,
Nor long as that fled bird to be.
I am unto my love the night,
I am her stone. I am her echoing tree.

*c.* 1950

## A Dream in Fever

Often we two, pleasant, alone
Walk in some wood divine.
The shadow stayeth by the stone
Thou tak'st my hand in thine.

I know not what words thou dost speak
Or I remember one
But everywhere our footsteps seek
Standeth at noon our sun.

Wanness is o'er and ruining pain
Like flowers the silence lies
As to our mortal loves again
List immortalities.

But a clock striketh. Ever I hear
The earth in her ring.
Thou art the dust, my dead, my dear
I to the dust coming.

1950

## The Church

She is a ship that doth enfold
The tempests in her hold.

She is an apse of angels grown
Out of a wayside stone.

She is a rose that will not rise
Save where a martyr lies.

She is a lantern that doth hide
Christ crucified.

1950

## Written in London

*(A lost poem remembered in a dream, 1.15 a.m., August 27th 1976, 26 years after composition.)*

O mountains immortal
Cradles of streams
The holds of eagles
Ye haunt my dreams;
All through the low summer
Through denied spring
Nevis, Nevis, bridebed of heaven
Beckoning.

1950


## Meadow Rain

Whene'er I heard the meadow rain
My heart had her old mood again
And high-head courage out did come
Following anew the fife and drum.
My flesh did make a merry din
Within my fine and extas'd skin.
All this because three raindrops flew
Over the shoulder of Loch Ewe.

But now I lie in city ways
And curse and rave the listless days
Rotting three times while waters fall
Out of the clouds, a sensual pall.
No lightfoot messenger have I
From hill or weir to bid me cry
'A thousand songs beset this hour
A thousand birds are in my power.'

89

O servile, deathly rain, go back
To the old impotent cloud-wrack
That gave thee birth, and say to send
One gold drop from the world's end
Touched by an osprey, nursed by air
That grew within some mountain's care
And I will grow and dream again
As when I heard the meadow rain.

? 1950


## Requiem for Dives

Sae routh, routh was your table
Ahint its yallow blinds.
Your guests in gowd and sable
Ne'er saw the lyart wynds,

Where your bairn watched hungert and nameless.
The sna' o' winter skies
Wither your sawle that, hameless,
Glowers into Paradise.

1950

# Harp Song for Alban

O if I dwelt again in Alban.
As the deer to the mountains,
As the berry to the rowan,
I shall return to Alban.

As the strings of the clairsach
To my heart are the glens of Alban.
O rocks, o rivers of Alban,
The sons of music.

Happy is the eagle of Beinn na Choireann
Upon his nest tonight.
Happy is the ouzel of Beinn a Ghloe
Upon his torrent tonight.
Happy is every bird that sleeps
Upon the hills of Alban.

O Alban, where I was born,
O Alban, where my harp first waked,
O Alban, where the sharp terns flew,
I shall return to Alban.

O that I danced again the swords in Alban.
O that I drank the milk of Glen na Alban.
O that I lay by Morar in Alban.
O Alban, my love.

Blessèd is the roe deer that steps in Glengeoullie
Never to leave there.
Blessèd is the trout that leaps by Caiplich
Ever to live there.
Blessèd is the child that plays by Eglis Colum
Whose children will lay his feet there.

Dark to me is summer and spring
Without the tongue of Alban,
Without the talking on the hills of Alban,
Without the high hills.

I shall return, my love Alban,
As the berry to the rowan,
As the deer to the mountains.
O if I dwelt again in Alban.

London 1950

## The Eagle to his Children

'The house that sleeps in Glen na h'Iolaire
 An old house stumbled, widowed, to the snows'
'I know it.
 Black stones. Haunted.'
                                    'No smoke blows.'
'The deer's moss grows unto the door'
'The weasel sleeps under the hearth.'
'The snow wind says the house-prayer on the floor.'
'No wife doth spin.
 No babe of Clann Ranald looks in.'
'O Ranald! Where is Clann Ranald! Alas the day!
 Landless, landless, children, vanished away.'

'The field that whispers in Glen na Chrudaire.'
'A shadow, no field! Who ploughs? What earthly
                                              hand?'
'A field once.
 No more. Desolate.'
                    'Our dear land
 That whispers still unto her own.'

'She sleeps not.' 'Her wan grasses cry
 And cry o'er centuries, deserts, the grave alone.
 No virgin sows
 No young man of Clann Alpin mows.'
'O Alpin! Where is Clann Alpin? Alas this day!'
'Landless, landless, children, vanished away.'

'The church that waits in Glen na Fada.'
'Ah, what church there? No church we ever crossed.'
'The roof's but a
 A sheep track's dust.
                          The gospel is lost.
 The grebe alone says "Agnus dei"'
'Dear is our eyrie in Glen no Fada.
 Dear is our blood. We'd shed it all for thee.'
'No bairn kneels there,
 No blood of Clann Sim ever.'
'O Sim! Where is Clann Sim? Alas this day!
'Landless, landless, children, vanished away.'

'My mountains, my beloved mountains!
 My empty glens, my sacred islands all
 The swans' holms.'
'The pochard's house.'
                          'Thou Halival,
 Where man alone may not tread.'
'What tears have your dark children now!'
'Now does your glory sleep among the dead.'
'No cradle have ye.
 No song, no minstrelsy.'
'Alas, my country! Alas! Alas this day!
 Perjured, perjured, thy children banished away.'

1950

93

## The Blessed Ones—The Wild Hawks

The poor hawks of the mountains
Are far more blessed than I,
For no man will bury them
When they come to die.
No man will shroud them
But the wild clust'ring sky
Will cover them with mercy,
The snow fall silently.

1950

## The Eve of St Mark

*In the Hebrides*
*(Opening of an Unfinished Poem)*

White with snow the hornèd peak.
White with hoary wind the sky.
No grebe waketh. The wild eider doth not speak
When Skidbladnir goeth by.
No solan doth arise. No seal awhile in all the islands doth sing.
The dead bell doth not ring.
The air alone knoweth silently, secretly,
The wan bell that striketh clear
This one even in the year
For the souls coming to Ygdrasil tree.

Who doth cross the aged sand,
Casting no shadows left nor right?
Look not, my life, tho' deathless beauty stand
Upon the seas of mortal sight.
No spar doth speak, no ship in any haven answer
Yon silver'd spar, yon dread spear,
The crew of yon fell glory. Cover your eyes.
These sails, ere the prime moon set,
Depart with the living, yet
No *De Profundis* but the silence rise.

Tis the Eve of St Mark.
The ghosts go in the world,
The great dead coming with Odin now. In his barque,
Like mail shining, like mists furled,
The dead go to host. To the dark machair in spirit
Those go by their own fire who sit.
Each by his lamp thinketh not of the rout,
But all this night hath beguiled
With many a fable his child,
And he shall die before the year is out.

Tis the Eve of St Mark.
Lest thou as Torquil Mor be,
From the black chimney let no fire spark.
Read in the holy breviary.
Let no fire spark. Odin upon the souls of men
Doteth, and can return again,
Again, again, cloaked in flame, on that chamber to look,
Where the sparks like souls flee.
Wouldst thou as Torquil Mor be?
Darken the house. Read in the holy book.

For the soul of Torquil Mor
*Miserere, Domine.*
This one even God did give unto the shore
To wed again the secret sea,
But thou believed'st it not, and a great feast on earth dressed.
Alas! Who came to thy feast?
Out of the machairs and the silences
Beyond Sule's Ness they came,
Thy guests sandal'd with flame,
By Asmundsvo, silent Rosmalaness.

1950


## The Poet's House

*(From* The Eve of St Mark.*)*

Now the sharded ashes drowse.
Holy Mark, thy candle lit,
Shine on my pen, my book, my life, this house,
Where no guests but the shadows sit.
By Christ alone, silent, relinquished,
Crouched on the cross, some light is sped.
Here are no guests and no loud harp doth moan,
But echoes, night, the dusks ever
Like a great cedar stir,
That stirs not by the crucifix alone.

1950

## Benighted in the Foothills of the Cairngorms: January

Cauld, cauld is Alnack. . .
Cauld is the snaw wind and sweet.
The maukin o' Creagan Alnack
Has snaw for meat.

Nae fit gangs ayont Caiplich
Nae herd in the cranreuch bricht.
The troot o' the water o' Caiplich
Dwells deep the nicht.

On a' the screes, by ilk cairn
In the silence nae grouse is heard,
But the eagle abune Geal Charn
Hings like a swerd.

Yon's nae wife's hoose ayont A'an
In the green lift ava
Yon's the cauld lums o' Ben A'an
Wha's smeek is sna.

A' the lang mountains are silent
Alane doth wild Alnack sing.
The hern, the curlew are silent.
Silent a' thing.

1950

# The Glen of the Clearance

Now the snows come to mass
And the white hares like ghosts pass.
*Asperges me, Domine.*

Wing and web behold the sky
And the wan whimbrel doth cry
*'Et clamor meus ad te veniat.'*

No fire shineth nor door doth stand
The reed prayeth in the land.
*'Exaudi nos, Domine.'*

No lamp showeth nor foot doth fall
And our fathers sleep, below the wall.
*'Kyrie eleison.'*

No sweet child here doth sing
But the poor lark to his King
*'Gloria in excelsis Deo.'*

And blinded bourne, fading field
Whisper where dormouse and owlet bield
*'Vitam venturi saeculi.'*

Land of our love, how thou did'st shine
Land of my heart, o never mine
*Dum recordaremur tui, Sion.*

Thou, not I, thou silent place
Shall speak the last word for my race,
*Sacrificium vespertinum*

'O Clan Domnuill, who shall rouse
The fire in the fallen house,
*Flammam aeternae caritatis?*

'Children of storm, who yet did see
In the guest the Blessed Trinity,
*Redime me, et miserere mei.*

'O Clan of Sim, whose ghosts yet light
Thy poet in the world's night
*Quorum memoriam agimus in terris*

'Feet of your children, did they but pass
The stones would shout in this frore grass
*"Sursum corda"'*

No voice answers. The great deer tread
Over the lands of the dead,
*Et dormiunt in somno pacis*

The peregrine has his eyrie above
But the children of Domnuill the world rove.
*Dimitte nobis debita nostra*

The hill hawk's eyas is cradled there
But the children of Sim where no man doth care.
*Libera nos a malo.*

The hill hawk's eyas beholds from heaven
Where the bread of the children to dogs was given.
*Libera nos, quaesumus, Domine*

c. 1950

99

# To Night

O house of heaven, come on thy western mountains.
O house of stars, the mountains wait for thee.
The white hare crouches down to welcome his beloved
   O night, come silently.

O house of night, thy pillars are the mountains
Soaring to meet thee. Here thy rooms are white
The great corries already long misted, silent.
   Come silently, O night.

O bearer of the birds of fierce Glamaig
O Staffa's, Eglis Colum's birds winging with thee
O bearer of the swan unto the reedy mountains
   O night, come silently.

O with the swans trav'ling from green Shieldaig
With the last swan of Sunart in thy flight
With the small birds that host upon the breasts of mountains
   Come silently, O night.

Roof of the eagle, roof of the wild children
Of Blaven on dark thrones awaiting thee
The kings throned in gold in halls of high Morven
   O night, come silently.

Already in their high places the kings are standing
In Torridon. Like stones, like gods upright
Who stared upon the sun are hooded before Hesper
   Come silently, O night.

O house of Canisp and of stark Suilven
The adder of Quinag creeps home to thee
With many a life that keeps in roots in lonely places
   O night, come silently.

For thee are the white canna lit, O stranger,
The fair ones. By still pools their tapers light
The farthest meads ever, the floors of the great mountains
Come silently, O night.

O house of music, when all else is silent
Save the high waterfalls, the western sea
Speaking in dusk, around the feet of island mountains
O night, come silently.

House of the exile, in his dreams ever
Coming by footless roads, in visions bright
All those in dreams who see their homes, their sweet summits
Come silently, O night.

O house of Columcille, who long by Uchd Ailiun
Soundly is sleeping, but did leave in thee
His songs, his psalms, his prayers, my joy upon the mountains
O night, come silently.

House of the Virgin, house of the great angels
Shelter thy poet and thy eremite.
Come, beauty of my life, upon the perfect mountains.
Come silently, O night.

1950

## A Gossip Silenced:
## The Thrush and the Eagle

'I keep the machair where
    The burnies gae'.
'I keep the mountain, bare
    O' a' but snae.'

'I see the rush steikin'
    My bonny nest.'
'I see the ray seekin'
    The amethyst.'

'I hae a muckle pea
    Inside my crap.'
'I hae twa maukins wi'
    A grouse on tap.'

'I hear the worms below
    The mole's bings.'
'I hear the whisprin' o'
    The aungel's wings.'

'I sit wi' merles a' day
    An' crack, an' a'.'
'I sit wi' cloods and say
    Naethin' ava.'

'I coont the lasses in
    The simmer leas.'
'I ken the Lord coontin'
    The centuries.'

by 1951

# All Sawles' Eve

I cam tae a yett in the derk hill
As I walked by my lane.
The reid roses were lauchin still
As in lang time gane.

As in lang time gane the reid rowan tree
Hung by the winnock fair,
And a bonny sang gaed thro the lea
In a' the lown air.

In a' the lown air whaur delicht did rove
I kent my ain name.
'My leal bairn, my dear luve,
My bairn come hame.

My bairn come hame, O lat me tak
Your haun' in my nieve.'
Ae step I took. The reidbreist spak
'O tis All Sawles Eve.'

O tis All Sawles' Eve, and didst thou come
Sae kindly aye, my ain?
I saw thro tears the warld toom
Whaur the bird sang his lane.

1951

# The Charity Child

O ye did glower on my bonny tune
And curse my hert's glee,
But the Haly Ghaist lichted doon
Amang the stour tae me.
Richt doucely, richt couthily,
Richt gently spak He.
'Bairn, tak yere shoon frae yon toon.
I'll walk the glens wi' ye.'

O saftly, like the lown wast, He cried
'I hae anither lea,
The water o' life tae bield beside,
A better hame for ye,
A' thing in My mercy,
A' thing gude and free,
Yere sangs, yere guide thro the warld wide,
My saikless aungels be.'

Lang as I wrocht for ye, ye showed
Nae kind luve tae me.
O I hae taen my leal road
O' sang and minstrelsy.
Sic joy, sic beauty
I never thocht tae be,
And a' thing keept by the luve o' God
Far, far frae herts like ye.

1951

# Sequence from 'The Ballad of Dhruimbogle'

Ca' up, ca' up, Lumlair an' Lumlain,
  Ca' up yer steeds sae free.
Ca' up, Brachbarns, yer muckle black rown
  Wi' the reid lunt in his e'e . . .

The doocit scraik, the cook out-shraik
  The wassail-hoose wa' cam' doon.
'Loup up, loup up,' the bairnies skirled
  Dhruimbogle's lap ower the mune.

He hadna ridden a mile, a mile
  A mile but barely three
When a' the clachan cam yammerin' oot
  Wi' bra clamjampherie.

Rant-boggle Bob an' Beamsie Tod
  An' Meezie wi' nae teeth,
An' Dugald hyowkit frae the rig
  Wi' stour aboot his claith,

An' craturs rinnin' in a shawl
  Wi' hoast and hirple sair
An' muckle sclaiter o' bauchle an' brogue
  Ca'd hind Dhruimbogle's mare.

Lasterns ther lowp an auld, auld man
  Wi' cranreuch in his e'en
An' och! for a' his banes were sair
  He sate him on a stane.

'But the gowd marys are wethered a'
  Och! o! leily la!
An' the reid rose fa's i' the mools sae fast
  I mayna see it fa'.'

An' they rade on, an they ramp on
    Were wonderly tae see
Til some drap doon in the grein lee loan
    An' trattled uncoly.

An' ower they linked an' aye they linked,
    Od's yett, but they linked sair
Until they cam' tae the Cauld Skerrie
    An' never linkit mair.

'O we hae cam tae the Cauld Skerrie
    Wi' the sules but and the sea
An' the win' blaws aff the Norland taps
    Sall never blaw mair on me.

'Ca' up, ca' up, Lumlair an' Lumlain
    Ca' up yer steeds sae free,
Ca' up, Brachbarns, yer muckle black rown
    Yese ride alane for me
O bield ye in yese guid grey maud
    An' ride frae Christ's countrie.

'O malisouns on the Cauld Skerrie
    An' the werwolf i' the faem.
An' ower they linked an' aye they linked
    An' they gaed linkin' hame.

Then up an' spak the braw Lumlair
    'O big ye a grey, grey stane
An' lay my guid braid sword abune
    An' the cross at my breist-bane.

'O lay my sword for hertes-heighth
    My cross for Christes dree,
An' I will speir a canny wee wind
    Unto God's ain ladye.

'"O bield us frae the lanely sea
  Creiplin' the craigs aboot,
An' whan we soom the sweir water
  O lat the starnies oot."'

An' syne ther cam' a white de'ils licht
  And syne ther cam a reid,
An' syne ther cam' oor ladyis licht
  An' they were sair afrayd.

Her blee was fayre, her e'en were rare,
  She was like snaw tae see.
She twined a kerchief on her gowd hair
  Gless-grein an' cramoisie.

'By rede, an' rood, an swevems guid
  I haud the wild sea-faem,'
An' they louted doon an' kissed her shoon
  An' ca'd tae Elfenhame . . .

An' she gaured hisht the wearie sea
  An' the mirk, mirk craigs aboot
An' whan they soomed the sweir water
  She lat the starnies oot.

1951

## Lazarus

'I hae nae road He didna ken
Whan He gaed in the warld wi' men.
His great ghaists walk in the weet,
In the sna', the sleet.

'Mercy is tint by storm and steep.
Justice is kisted leagues deep.
His wings are my ainly hoose,'
Said puir Lazarus.

1949–51


## Lat my demon be

In my chaumer wauks the bird
O' eternity.
Lat him sing tae me.
Frae my he'rt, this cauld yird,
Springs his gowden tree,
But ye loe it not.
O ye weary o't.
Ay ye carp o' walth alane.
Whil ye carp, in vain, in vain,
Derkness fa's, my bird is gane
*Lat my demon be*

1949–51

## The Poet in the Dark Church

Look not upon the candle's flame
Look at the little mouse that came
Happily, happily finding what
But for the light he seeth not.

He hath his supper and is gone
Whilst thou, poor fool, still starest on,
And all thy pride and all thy art
Bring only shadows to thy heart.

1954

## The Poet II

In this poor room the wine is dry
The ember is dead
And one bright star silently
Lights the sleeper's head.

Hunger's grey band halted stand
Tho' the door swings ajar
And the page by the sleeper's head
Answers the star.

by 1954

## The Poet III

Go to bed, my soul,
When the light is done.
Sleep from enemies
Blanketed in bone.

Let thy blood grow cold
As a mouldering stone
On a martyr's tomb,
Known to God alone.

On the stair of truth
Down and up are one.
Bless the cobbled street
When the light is gone.

When the light is past
When the flower is shown
Let the poet be
Common earth and stone.

by 1954

## The Poet IV

Pity him not. He wishes nought
But his own sacred thought.

The poems from his strange glory pour
As withered leaves, no more.

Or they are candles which shall light
Others to his dark night,

Along all common lanes to be
Sconces of mystery

Yet by his own door never shall blow
. One sconce, but winter snow,

Who thinks all figures, beauties blent
Are prisons where he went.

His rose transcends all roses dim,
Shining past art for him.

What is not light, what is not rose
He knows it not and knows

He hears upon the cobbled street
The Holy Virgin's feet.

by 1954

## The Poet's Hours

I have no dial and no glass
My time is measured high above
The silent stars that pray and pass
Before my ghostly Love

For one star of them all, unlike
All other stars will shine for me
When the great clock of Heaven will strike
*Angelus Domini*

undated, listed by 1954

## Prayer to the Virgin

O Bethlehem,
Beauty of Bethlehem,
Never forget me.
Never let me forget thee.
Holy Lady, bend over the manger and bless me.
Pray for me.
Cover me with the roof of peace.
Tho' the world dwell with me,
As the hill thrush make me free.
In snows, in winds, in danger,
Thou great angel, come in brightness to me.
Light the road for me.
Fountain of felicity,
Bend over thy Child and bless me.

Inverness-shire 1952


## The Franciscan

He walks beside a river where
A few wind-stunted osiers tress,
Sagely within a wood of prayer,
Silently through the silences.

Over his head a common vine
Turns the true Cross. The earthly sod
Bleeds with the passion-flowers that shine
In transepts of his thoughts of God.

1952

## What wilt Thou do with this dry heart?

What wilt Thou do with this dry heart
From which no powers or beauties start?
Here the invisible dark grief
Turns all to dust, blossom and leaf.
A forlorn roadway I am grown
A beggar's purse, a sloe, a stone.

I am all things of essence sour,
Empty or dry as this drab hour
Which stands upon my blood and bears
Only strong languors for its heirs
And pestilences, death and need
Save those it has no other seed.

1952-3


## The Poet V

When shall I come to Thy abode,
So welcoming, so kind?
I have come by a weary road
Thro' desperate chance and wind,

By hovels, shadows, miseries when
I see Thy footstep plain
Under the lampless homes of men
And in the homeless rain,

And there, O Christ, Thy words start
Where silent doorways be,
Making a lantern of my heart
That I shall never see.

1953

## To Sir Winston Churchill on entering
## his eightieth year

Thou hast no age who wert our royal day
Risen on all men's hearts, our hope that stood
Making our streets as towers when towers lay
Shattered in dust and the dust quenched with blood.
Churchill, upon thy name our loves yet shine
From Narvik, Libya, Crete, where'er they be,
Under the sands of Dunquerque, in the Rhine
By Anzio, Arnhem, in the dangerous sea
Our mystery past all years, with thee, with us,
Built in one bastion out of wounds and stress
Singular in the world our holy house
Signed with the hand of everlastingness.
Who is its poet? Thou, past counterfeits
'Til words are ships and landing-grounds and streets.

November 1953


## The Little Waterhen

*A fairy tale for grown-ups*

The little waterhen crept into the rushes to die.

As the sun set over the river it seemed to the shabby bird that she had come to a great archway, and the spirit of air and waters waited for her there.

'What story have you to tell, little bird?' he asked.

'I lived all my life in the old wild orchard called Broad Lay on the bank of this mountain river, and there a lonely ill-cared for child used to come, who had never seen goodness in the world, but only hardship and hate. There in Broad Lay everything was still as a church. Only in the cherry trees the wren sang "Laudamus Te".'

'And who else came into this poor place?'

'An old tired woman used to come with her wash-tub and a bundle of heavy plough clothes which she washed beside the river. Sometimes she smiled and nodded and spoke merrily to the child, but he only scowled at her in suspicion, and wished her away, and climbed up higher into the tree. Yet whenever the old woman smiled and nodded to him, it was as if the trumpets of angels called through the green orchard "Benedicamus Te".'

'And up in the high tree the child sat each day, for his body ached from blows, so that he wished only to crouch in the fork, eyes shut in weariness like a stone child, half hidden among the leaves. And presently pain left him. Some blackbirds scuffled in the wall of black hollies, and the horned cattle passed below him to drink, and it seemed to him that he heard all these simple creatures say in the silence "Adoremus Te".'

'And all this time I myself was sitting on a nest in the marsh-marigolds, and one day the eggs chipped, and I had eight water chicks. They were scarcely much bigger than bumble bees, and when they were tired I would call "Notch. Notch. Notch," and they would all run out of the pool under my wings. The child followed us about the river bank in joy and amazement.

'"She is like a little house. She is a little home. She is brave and good. See how she shelters them and pities them. That is true goodness. I have never seen anything so beautiful in all my life.

That is how it should be in the world." All at once the marigolds opened their hearts to the full sun, whispering "Glorificamus Te".'

'You have done a great work in the world, little black water-hen,' said the spirit.

'But I have not told you all. In her cottage on the sandbank above the river the poor old woman died, and was buried and forgotten. Only the wandering child remembered her gnarled hands and wept for pity in the green orchard. "One day I shall do some good in the world to brave old hands like these."'

It seemed to the dying bird that the golden arch of the air and water burst into music 'Gratias agimus Tibi propter magnam gloriam Tuam'.

In the rushes the eyes of the little waterhen closed.

1953


## An Ancient Cathedral

I was builded high,
Builded by the dead,
Builded to the sky,
Blessed to hold the Bread,

Where a child who owns
Neither crust nor crumb
Kneels upon my stones,
Sees the world to come,

Knows me bent above
His cold want at last—
Me the glory of
Future, present, past—

And is builded high
One with all the dead,
Builded to the sky
Past the bonds of bread.

by 1954

## Invocation to Our Lady

Thou above my heart,
Thou above my pen,
Blessed Star of silence,
That shinest on men,

Thou did'st bear the Tree
In thy earthly sod,
The autumn of the angels,
The ripening of God.

O tower perpetual
Whose stairs of delight
Transcend from star to star
And from night to night,

Come, ensomb'ring Love
On my life, my pen,
The autumn of the angels,
Of the dreams of men.

by 1954

# Birth of Our Lady

Cherubim and Seraphim
Cedars of Lebanon
A little girl
A little girl
A little girl was born
Where there are angels on the rooftops
And songs upon the morn
In the barren land of Israel
Our Lady she was born.

Cherubim and Seraphim
Cedars of Lebanon
A tiny cry
A tiny cry
A tiny cry at night
Where the rivers run in whispers
Where the prophets sound with might,
In the holy land of Israel
Came the Mother of the Light.

Cherubim and Seraphim
Cedars of Lebanon
A prophecy
A prophecy
A providential call
Where the stars run through the darkness
Where a child will fill a stall
In the ancient land of Israel
Came the Mother of us all.

by 1954

## Song of the Bad Hat

I don't want money until I'm dead.
I've a mother with money clinking in her head,
Ha'pennies in her heart and pennies in her bed,
And she dances in diver's boots of lead.

I want the moon. I want to be
As high as the blue hare, happy and free
As the grasses of Parnassus that smile on me
In the hills past use and usury.

You can keep my hat. You can pawn my coat.
Let the road be my roof, my landlord a stoat.
O never do my hangdog angels gloat
On the holy picture of a five pound note.

Rags! Rags! Blessèd be rags!
Blessed be holes in stockings and hags
With prams full of sticks in the mountains of the stags
In the golden hills beyond moneybags.

Out goes my mother, out like a light,
To shepherd her farthings home from sight,
From the wolves and the wantons and the wrong and
                                        the right
And she folds them deep in the night of night.

I cannot know where the farthings rest.
God cannot go where they lie in her breast,
But God is away with the hags and the rest
Of the prams and the sticks in the hills of the west.

I don't want money until I'm dead.
Then the pennies will lie on my eyes like lead,
So spend them, my love, on a cuppa or a bed
When my last sun's risen and my last song said.

February 1954

## Thought of the Bad Hat

O the parents blew up and the rains blew down
Beside the divorce court door
And the orphans blow like leaves through the town
Ten a penny or more.

And I sing to them 'O my loves you must be
As thick as birds on the bough,
All dancing devilish hats like me
For no man loves you now.'
    And the sick girls go like birds in the snow
    And sad boys go to gaol.

Your father's shutters are dark and down
    And your mother's candle fades,
As they lie with their loves in the cobbled town
    And all the hearts are spades
O your fathers lie with their loves below
    And mothers lie . . .
To bury you deep, deep, deep, heigh-ho
    Where the stars of mercy . . . faid

      And the sick girls go like birds in the snow
      And the wide boys die in gaol

      And all the lamps of earth are out
      And all the hearts are spades . . .

1954

## An old Wife hates me

An old wife hates me and she would
Send her sour spears upon my heart,
But my forefathers from the mountains start,
The glum ghosts in the solitude,

Sombring me as the mother wren
Sombres her blind and helpless young,
And the old carping bitter tongue
Bites on, but bites itself again.

London 1954


## The Last Eagle

Turn, o eagle, in thy gyre,
Where the mountains shine,
Thong'd with silence and with fire
On thy heart and mine.

Turn, beloved, turn.
Sense and shadows fold,
And the wind grows cold,
Tho' the mountains burn.

Turn. Capella on thy breast
Does but darken mine.
All the wanderers are at rest
Let the mountains shine.

1954

# Anima

My thoughts go where no ray will rouse
Half-heard, unknown, within the deeper house
Peering and startling by the gates of sight
As they were stars and I were night.

But when I look not for them more
They break untimorous thro' wall and floor,
The unknown suns and swans and splendours bright
'Til I am stars and they are night.

1954

# The Writer to the Reader

Still on my words the ghost must float
Betwixt us two insensibly
And you shall read here what I wrote
And all you write for me.

So in my poor street is your home
Risen amid my silent thought
And to its door your love will come
Altho' I knew him not.

1954

*Hospital in London—*
*and Recovering in the North*
*1956–1966*

## To Poetry: written in hospital

O my heart, O my light
Bowed before thy gate at last
In the darkest hours of night
O my beauty never past,

Never fail, thou ever free
Never living but for me.
Thou my sad satiety
Go in light and dark with me.

Go, my angel, treading through
Every mist of human thought.
By my sacred fountains grow
Flowers my bitter tears have brought

O my heart, O my light
Lead me to my own at last
Thou my day and thou my night
Stay until the day be past.

? 1956


## Where are the holy angels

Where are the holy angels that were here
Dwelling upon the walls of wit and sense
The guests of every ghostly rampart where
…. …. …. …. …. innocence

Where are the scrolls of the ineffable
Now written? In some vacant land below
The wing, the web, the scale, the secret seal
Between the progenies where our beauty     grow

Where are my angels that they lean no more
Upon the bridge of stillness, while I move
Dissatisfied, a wanderer on some shore
Of oceans never charted . . .

1956

## In Sickness

By my remembered words
That let me pray
In my poor body let them stay
As the bright noise of singing birds
That sing at birth and death of day.

So may I conjure dawn
Even unto this night,
So think my heart by her own light
Shall rise and wash upon this lawn
And come with slow steps to thy sight.

28 May 1956

## Let there be no more angels

Let there be no more angels in the night
    When the soul keeps house.
Gone the white Sun, the white satyrion,
    No elegiac flower could ever light
That darkness, nor should rouse
The dread and complete silences that lie
Over this heart that knew Persephone
    And sleeps regretless in strange hostelries.

1956–61


## Envoi

Wren upon the green tree,
Snowdrop on the green,
And all things on earth
Seen and unseen,

Bend before the sweet Ghost
In the hearts of men,
And their heavenly Father
Bless again.

Chaffinch on the green tree,
Small, immaculate,
Sole, unseen by all men
Singing late;

Snowdrop in the green wood
Like the light of thought,
That without that lantern
Lighteth naught;

All my gentle children
Journey home with me
Unto God our Father
Constantly.

1956

## I have no song

I have no song, but turn to my great Light
Where death and life are images, where nothing
Of either stayeth as a tokening
Unto the dust. O I was once the night
Around the Invisible, once the ecstasy
Built into God. To Him my wounds now fly
Through sickness, sadness, silences, slow hours
My bridges of insensate mystery.
As songs they tremble from earth's fading towers
To stars that darken to eternity.

c. 1956

# The Poet to the Holy Ghost

Here my weary sense doth lie
And maketh for Thy wings a sky.
Here is no sweet poetry
Nor star, my Lord, to welcome Thee,
But empty night, where thou must range
Ghostly Thyself, this ghost to change.
Naught is beautiful, naught is free.
Hunger and the world slay me.

Here in this dragon's garden, sown
By moonlight is a thought of stone,
Nourished in my deadly airs
Of languors, fevers and despairs.
Here like wildfire Tophet roars,
Lazarus dieth of his sores
And the accursed figtree shows
Cold as Ygdrasil, fruits of snows,
While thou goest equally
I and the world ruin me.

Here do my earthly loves all look
Abstracts from a magician's book.
Truth is lost. His angels mime
In the dancing-house of time.
When thou didst shield and succour me
Thousands were as unity
Now disparity is all.
One is fled to several,
And I feel the fatal kiss
Of Satan out of the abyss.

Only Thou, my lord, wilt light
Upon this ant-heap of old night,
Search and find within this mess
Of mists knitted with nothingness.
O keep Thy *Dies Irae* yet
Until some concord here is set,
But come, Thou heavenly housewife, come
With Thy glory, with Thy broom.
Sweep and clean incense this house.
*Veni, Creator Spiritus*.

1958-61

## Sequence from 'Tigers'

When I put out this rushy light
Tigers will stalk the house all night . . .

The light is out. The bath tap drips.
The tigers yawn and lick their lips.

I cannot think of toast going brown,
The water-hen's wedding, the magic town,

The unborn boys who lie asleep
In windfall pears in orchards deep.

Only I hear, 'Beware! Beware!
Of Bengal tigers on the stair,

The old ravine, the lonely note,
Indus and Ganges in its throat',

'Til every wind on window pane
Has the tiger's voice again.

1957-58

## When I shall die / The Lost Sense

When I shall die, let there be mountains near.
The milk-white ptarmigan, the wand'ring deer.
When I shall die, let the poor dipper call
Out of her foothills by the waterfall.

O let no human, festering, hating heart
Come in that place with ignorance or art.
Let there be none to mock my life with words
But the bare mountains and the calling birds.


[See that. I'm not dead in spite of you all.]


### The Lost Sense

Where has gone my happy harp?
In some hospice of the brain.
In some dark street of the sense
Nevermore to harp again.

Nevermore on earth to be
Like the green reed in the rain.
Like the green finch in the tree.
Nevermore again.

c. 1958–61

# Lines Written after a Nervous Breakdown
## (I)

I have forgotten how to be
A bird upon a dawn-lit tree,
A happy bird that has no care
Beyond the leaf, the golden air.
I have forgotten moon and sun,
And songs concluded and undone,
And hope and ruth and all things save
The broken wit, the waiting grave.

Where is that mountain I must climb
To gain again some common time,
Not this stayed clock-hand that must be
Some foretaste of eternity?
Where is that task or terror that
Will wake a slow magnificat
From this dead sense, from these dull eyes,
That see no more to Paradise?

There is no night so deep as this
Inevitable mind's abyss,
Where I now dwell with foes alone.
Feather and wing and breathing bone
And blessed creatures come not here,
But the long dead, the aguish fear
Of never breaking from this hold,
Encapsuled, rapt, and eras old.

There is no second of escape.
As with some forest-wandering ape
Whose sad intelligence may go
So far and nevermore may grow,
I am enchained most subtly by
A thousand dendrons 'til I die,
Or find my mountain, storm and shock
This graven hour and start the clock.

September 1964

# Lines Written after a Nervous Breakdown
## (II)

Come, lamefoot brain, and dance and be
A merry carnival for me.
We are alive in spite of all
Hobgoblins who our wits did call.
With ghosts and gallowsbirds we went
Hundreds of leagues 'til, fiercely spent,
We laid ourselves to weep and cry
Beyond the house of memory.

We have been lepers, and now run
To sit again within the sun,
And smile upon some country fair
With Punch and poor dog Toby there.
We, who did only think to die
Now laugh and mock the revelry.
Up, barefoot brain, and fill your hall
With flags as for a festival.

Yet you are poor and slow to do
The blessed things I ask of you,
Haunting with spectres still and still
Remembering your dungeon's chill,
Where you did cower and aye did grow
A frenzied circus for your foe,
Who sought you in the blood's dim arc,
And in the night–time, in the dark.

Peace, friend, and think how we are here
Through dangers, desolations, fear.
We two alone, now all is o'er
Will never move from pleasure more.
We two will sit like birds i' the sun
And preen and pipe while others run
And straddle in the world's proud play.
We have been night, who now are day.

October 1964

133

# To a Hazel Twig

Shalt thou have blessedness of air
While I have none? O shalt thou know
The breath of mountains everywhere
While I lie in the grave below?
Rather than that, o let me be
A wren-trod twig upon a tree.

Or I will mix with fire and go
Unto the great hills all my own,
Changed, ashen, seeking but the snow
And the white ptarmigan alone,
That with the storms and bents and winds
I will live still with living minds.

I care not if I die, but care
For the long cities of dead men.
Let me not be enclosed there
Useless, but let me be again
As gossamer outside the byre
Or a dry gean-log for a man's fire.

I fear the dead men from some old
Strange memory of childhood's gloom.
Their silent stones my dreams enfold
And trap and hide me in their tomb.
I would not lie with them, but be
A tide-hued bone within the sea.

O bird, or wave, or blessed pine
Forget not me, thy sister here,
Let me be part of ye to shine
And dance and glimpse for many a year,
So in sad wastes I come not by
But still by nests, and brinks, and sky.

November 1965

# The Solace of the Other World

*for Lena Stuart*

A world goes by among the mountains
As the wind goes by,
A throng who know nothing of my dreams
Nor whether I live or die

And are so dear in their uncaring,
Bent on their quests, that I
Am solaced by this intent world
And my immunity

From being ever bedevilled, questioned
By curlew, or grebe or pie
In the lands among the mountains
Where winds breed and cry.

O sleep, come to me this night as softly
As the hay that grows nigh
The snow-line whispers above some heart
Crouched in its cavity.

*c.* 1966

# To a Pheasant

When I am all forgotten
With eel and ouzel and bee,
And the dark wood has thy buried breast
And some dark rock has me,

O shall we both inhabit
Some other almonry
As merry as when we loved here
The spring, the green pine tree?

And shall we quest in quiet there
Thro' all our new country
Without the sundering stiles of sense
To lie 'twixt me and thee?

I know not, but I linger
In my dry path to see
This tussock and this red, red bird,
As all were kin to me.

c. 1959, revised c. 1966

*The 'Wonderful Years'*
*Aberdeen : Hospital and Holidays*
*1970–1973*

## Prayer to a Tree

I am the dark and twilit one.
I am the absence of the sun
The presence of the antic moon
Of things that were, and shall be soon.

But this proud bough beside my face
Has life and power and love and grace.
I am the shadow, she the thing.
Within her height the wild birds sing.

And I stay here beside her as
Each trembling ray and light she has
Could light my darkness, quench my want,
Fill me anew, like Hellespont,

With all I am not and would be.
The golden day, the journeying sea.
Dear bough of this sweet wood renew
The shivering husk that clings to you.

before 1970

## To A.M.J.

Long is the road to the mountains
Long thou art dead.
I climb each meanest staircase
Seeking thy bed,

To wake thee and bring thee in beauty
Home to thy door,
That the dish and the book and the firelight
Shine as before.

These were poor forms which thy love made
Lovely for me.
Long is the road and the seeking
My Love, for thee.

Long is the road to the mountains
No kestrels weep.
I have no home where thou art not
No bread but sleep.

Undated ? 1970

## The Artist

I must pursue my lonely way
Unto Antares, under the earth,
Unto the waters under the ground,
To magnitudes, to dearth.

No one shall journey where I tread,
Nor kindest friend nor cruellest foe.
Alone I came into the world
Alone I still must go.

Take me not from this silent art
Of lonely strengths, that bind me fast
The estuaries, the wild drake's cry,
My future and my past,

Or thou shalt find that I am dust
That thou hast got, a mote, no more;
But leave me to my own, and I
Shall lean, a lover, by thy door.

21st October 1970

# The Dead

Tonight the dead come in their masque
Out of the coigns where they have grown
Lovely, distinct, personal, alone.
Now from his place does a dead man ask

'What of the ship I rigged for thee,
A trembling child?' 'Another morn
Took away my ship, her striped sails borne
Afar, my pride, my agony;

'For I never forgot her sailing more
Staunch to the storms, the turning foam,
And I hoped some happy child would come
And find my ship on some other shore.

'This was the thing thou did'st for me
And for thy soul that still does ride
A beauty within my life's fast tide.
She is thy immortality.'

Tonight the dead crowd. Rosy and bright
An old ghost gleams, a shepherd who gave
Sixpence, before he stooped down to the grave,
To a country child on a Saturday night.

Thy silver, old man, bought sweet on sweet.
So long it is spent, yet never spent,
So often it comforts the cold world's lent
And I see thy smile on the lamp–lit street.

This dark shawled spirit had scarce a crumb
On earth, a dusting of tea, but set
A feast for guests in finery met
On a New Year's night in her poor ben room;

And I see again the flagon, the grate
Of burning pine-cones, the short-cake, the cream
Bought by fast and striving and dream,
The calico dress a costume of state,

Poor majesty for a night, thy eyes
Fiery as eagles out of the isles
Shine on me yet in the darkened miles
That lie between here and Paradise.

Tonight the dead come thronging apace,
Patient, perfect, splendid, alone.
Who long since builded in vision and bone
Their work and parted to their place.

26th October 1970

## To a Friend, Bereaved

I would take thy thoughts on me,
Sweetest friend, to lighten thee.
But I cannot. But I cannot.
I can never, never be
Thy deep diffuse identity.

I would walk from shore to shore
Turnpikes, continents and more.
'Twould not help. 'Twould not help.
At each step the soul's shut door
Lies 'twixt us two for evermore.

At each step I further go
In secrecy and storm and snow
Of my own, of my own.
None can serve but what below
Thee lies in darkness 'til it grow,

And it may grow a gracious tree
To shield thyself but never me.
We are two lives. We are two lives.
All I can do is wait to be
Spectator of divinity.

12th December 1970

## To Dinah and Ronnie Garden: At Night

My thoughts at eve that come to me
What potent triremes of the mind are ye
Bearing each in his shape
From isthmus and dark'ning cape
Eternity.

And I would light the little light
And lie awhile within my homely chair
Staying, with plate and pen
Your misty navies again
And what sails there:

All my quenched hopes, disastrous hours
And harassment and hunger, chidden powers,
Homelessness, go at last
Where a mere candle doth cast
Its light in showers.

Lo, I defeat ye utterly
Sometimes at dusk, however mighty ye be
The old fleet of the soul,
Where a friends' gift keeps whole
Substance in me.

16th December 1970


## An Experience

Sometimes upon some silent street
A passer-by will say to me
'You, the stranger whom I meet
Are come to take my own from me,
My safety and my soft retreat.'

What is this thing? I do not know
This brawler, nor have seen before
His face, for with my songs I go
Unseeing, maybe by his door,
And now he melts my lines like snow;

And they are gone and I am left
With this outraged, contorted man,
And both of us besieged, bereft
For some dark reason that I can
Never trace to its hiding-cleft.

Is it his soul that he doth see
And hate to see within my look,
A much-scrawled sheet, a tragedy,
The peril of some traveller's book
Who has come close to death to be

At last upon that city lane?
Or is it some more earthly thing,
Poor shoes, poor raiment, world's disdain
Shown in my mended covering
That minds him on the dust again?

Or is it something dire in me
That looks upon him I see not
But that all other men must see
And shrink to see, some flaw, some rot
Within the soul's wide mystery?

I do not know, but know we who
Confront upon that quiet street
Among the churchbells and the dew
Are enemies from the hour we meet,
And I dread him and his thoughts too.

18th December 1970

## The Unwanted Child

I was the wrong music
The wrong guest for you
When I came through the tundras
And thro' the dew.

Summon'd, tho' unwanted,
Hated, tho' true
I came by golden mountains
To dwell with you.

I took strange Algol with me
And Betelgueuse, but you
Wanted a purse of gold
And interest to accrue.

You could have had them all,
The dust, the glories too,
But I was the wrong music
And why I never knew.

26th January 1971

## To London

I come to thee from sweeter dawns
And from a fairer love.
I have known the departure
Of the last star above
Ben Dearg and Sgurr na Gillean
When no mouse doth move.

Here I have but a hearthless room,
A shaking window frame
And a rended roof over my head
—'Tis all on earth I claim—
But the great hills still wait for me
And call me by my name;

For my name is as old as the rock's blood
And they and I are one,
Only dark Algol, the Pleiades,
And Pegasus alone
Looked on the world to shine on us
When we should be begun.

Tonight the night wind blows over Glen Brittel
The peregrine stoops no more,
Shuttered behind her eyes' thin membrane.
Shadows sleep on the floor,
But from every shadow and cranny
My own watch evermore.

I am not away when absent.
When absent, I am still
Walking the wild ledges,
The saddlebacks until
Each root, each whitening water
Rises upon its hill.

What canst thou do to defeat her . . .
Blaven . . . this winter's night?
Thou hast nought but a lean cat
Below a neon light,
The tide keeping the cold steps,
The buoys burning bright,

Marking the empty channel
Where the ship goes down
Between the blinded windows
Of all the footless town.
I shut my eyelids. Behind them
A cloud forms like a crown.

27th January 1971

## To Roman Stamm

O roof of the fragrant fire,
Be thou a memory to me on the roads.
O child's grace in an antique language said
Lighten all loads

I bear within this sore world.
Feast of that house with such high beauty given
I do not ask for any hostel more
Who dined in heaven.

13th February 1971

## To a New Friend

What if I see in thee more than thou art,
I see within myself what I may be,
A road as yet untrod, a mystery,
Because thy mystery invades my heart

And steals upon it with the forms of towers
And streets and castellated houses graced
With lovers' candles in their windows placed,
And all these signs do draw my earthly hours

To fashion now the road that never was
Within my days to come unto your door
By many an orchard never seen before.
By many a hazel wood I come because

Thou hast some little look that speaks unto
The ghost behind the soul, the inmost vein
Of sense, and tho' I never come again
I shall have seen by selves I never knew.

22nd February 1971

## The Fire of Apple Wood

In thee the secret orchards blow
And put their ultimate apples forth
To nurture me amid the snow
And in the gorgeous north.

The north falls with his green light round
My shaking life and I would glide
Like a lost seed into the ground
And there in chills abide

With buried summers, but thou hast
This latest fate and trick to be
The golden cloak that shelters last
Me and my poetry.

Sweet tree, I watch thee 'til thou art
But embers in my bushman's stove
And for thy company does my heart
Seek now her rest in love.

3rd April 1971

## The Philistine

You did translate my thoughts
Into another coin,
Putting a worth on these
That I could never join

To any membrane of dream—
Halfpence, and pence, and pounds
Won from some holy summit,
Torn from some ghostly grounds;

And so you keep for ever
Your hopeless load of loss,
While I keep the misty river
And never venture across.

Our blood's old history to both
From the same chasms fell,
But I find the meadows of heaven
Where you, I think, find hell.

Ah, but some star, some wind,
Some unknown thing flies o'er
That keeps for ever betwixt us
This thin but keyless door.

11th April 1971

## The Corner Shop

This poor, pared life where I must fight
For every crust, it seems no life at all,
And I would rather watch the candle light
My face turned to the wall,
And go without the milk, the meal, the bread,
In the dark shop filled with the walking dead.

For tho' I die, I have a dream
Of rich contentment in the silence here.
Tho' all my food is shadows, yet I seem
Far from the whole world's fear
In some great music where the ghosts yet pace
And bless and bow a hand's breadth from my place.

Yet I must stir. Some last voice cries
With earthly meaning to the life within
To shed the quilt of newspapers and rise
And come unto my kin,
The anxious, wary, superficial hosts
Within the corner store, and leave the ghosts.

But they are never to be left,
And their high powers are now a calm in me
Deserting not. I am no whit bereft.
As the herb trinity
Such hours sweeten long upon my sense.
I buy a loaf and thank my Providence.

11th April 1971

## On Remembering an Attic Room
## in London

That life of hungry days was remedied
By long feasts of the mind,
And in the stoveless twilight did I find
Eternity and the fast-buried seed
That yet would grow an arbour. There did wind

A rose at last that blew above my pain
As earthly roses can
Smell best unto some waif, some weary man,
In a closed court blown on by night and rain.
O thou bare room, I would have thee again.

151

I shall ne'er know that darkliest plant to climb
Ten stages o'er my head
Within this safe and softly-sheeted bed.
No passages there are from here thro' time
Magnificent, uncaring for my rime,

As I cared not, but still remember all
The obscure way I went,
The sickness and the power, the soul intent
To come at last to where it must, the call
Of that which made my want a festival.

12th April 1971


## A Wish

Let me be as the moonlight that seeks out
The sleeping face,
Behind whose bones lie all the clamorous rout
Of thoughts within their place

Trancèd and caught as they would never move
From their locked door,
That I may light men's future with my love
Softly as I pass o'er.

7th May 1971

## To Christa Ahrens

Maybe I ceased to grow at where thou art.
Maybe beneath the iron mountain lay
Sleeping the many flowers of my heart
That could not raise their heads nor yet decay

Wholly below the inescapable
Dark dearth of all that came upon my youth.
I have not loved the old. I never will
See in their creeping dreams one shape of truth;

But thou dost come, gold-headed, to my door
And straight I know the gentle things I had
So long ago by my sweet brook before
It came to join the torrent of the mad

Indefinite world. I look at thee and feel
Stirring the speedwell and the violet
Out of their starved night and lustres steal
From a blest dawn that joins our ages yet.

Maybe I died long since at where thou art,
And maybe thou shalt die as I did too,
Unable to withstand the closèd heart.
But stay, this hour, gold-headed, in the dew.

8th May 1971

153

## On an Old Woman Sleeping
## in Hospital

Within this carven ear, shut eye,
I see the hurrying world go by.

In this old shrunken thing is dressed
Man's first dream and his lastliest.

So at the sleeper's side I write
Figures and canticles of light,

And spy and smile upon her ease—
Tell-tale of all her mysteries.

The sun's beam moves, as still I guess
Who answers 'No' and who says 'Yes,'

And in what turret thought must stay
To search and visit in our day

Out of the marches of the light
Beyond the lands and keeps of night.

Hours crawl like blindworms as I dream
Who wrought *that* work, *that* sense, *that* theme.

And who and who and who must sleep
In the steep artery and deep

Mysterious calyx of her brain
Upon some noon to rise again,

And walk, eyes downcast, in our world,
Sombre and strange, a thought half-furled,

To turn, entranced, to his own
Still house, where all flowers are unblown.

O thou unborn, who never quite
Say 'Yes' to day and 'No' to night

Thou loveliest guest of all I see
In this old woman's mystery.

1971

## The Two Senses of Life

Two separate senses fall from night and day,
And one is sole and individual,
Pure as the starlight, whilst the other may
Be broken as by hasty feet that fall
On the stone causeway underneath my wall.

One is the sure great constancy of dream
To which I came I scarce know how but know
That it was through the interspersèd stream
Of the other broken one in which I go
On common errands in the street below.

6th June 1971

# The Grey Goose Skein

I am not your kind, kind of the skies.
I am different, far,
Yet some wild part of me rises and flies
With you by some cold star,
Leaving my own,
Unlov'd, alone.
I must go wherever the grey goose cries.

I must hasten wherever you speak,
Yet I am not of those
Who after human discourse seek—
'How the long day goes
Heavily and with pain
Unto evening again!'—
I must listen for rivulet and creek

Putting forth their old loves once more
Tho' those travellers know nought of me
And will pass in music o'er
This heart utterly
Ignoring it as tho'
It were but lichen below
That flight that it must follow and still adore.

And if you knew of me, o grey goose skein,
You would fly more high,
The wind-breaker pierce unto the steepest lane
Of the last sky,
Troubled, vociferous,
Wiser than us
Who dream and love and kill again.

I would not kill, o wedged peers,
Yet I would not have you
Trust me and my wandering verse.
Your true friends are few
And are despised of men,
Refused, murdered again
Each day of life by kinsmen murderers.

16th July 1971


## The Adder of Quinag

The grey roots circle thee, who never knew
At any hour within thy travels lone
A human shape but mine. Thou com'st to view,
Wild, unafraid, what stands beside thy stone
And gazes on thee in thy wilderness
Of fifty miles. What thinkst thou of me,
For I am of a race thou could'st not guess
Would murder all thy hapless innocency?

O mountain, take thy small heart back again
And keep him in thy care when I shall go,
Unvisited by all things but the rain,
The hurtless sunbeams, and the winds that blow
For ever in his moors. O let him hold
No intricate memory of that being who stood
Just once by his wild beauty, and did fold
Him with a blessing alien to my blood.

21st August 1971

# I should not leave this green earth

I should not leave this green earth
With joy, but joy grows rare
Among the cruelties, grudges,
The murdering words said there
The denial of the bright heart,
Nurture of care.
I would not leave this lovely land
But love goes elsewhere.

I cannot live without love,
The white and gentle star
That rose on the wood of infancy
Still shines, tho' now afar.
O never eclipsèd, immortal
That no change can mar,
It yet lights me, but lights also
The weapon and the scar.

The dagger wears now a sharper edge
Thro' many thrusts ta'en.
I scarce remember love more
When I see it again.
I haste not to the high passes
But keep the weary plain,
For I have almost forgotten love
And all things save pain.

So I must travel from this stage
And keep a vigil where
Love will come, or will not come,
If anything comes there;
But I will have night or delight
My quiet bed to share.
I would not leave this lovely earth
But love goes elsewhere.

1st October 1971

## Misgivings

This gift doth seem thy outward love and yet
This love is in my heart, but scarce in thine.
'Tis my desire for love, so desperate set
On sere shores where for it I long did pine.

O cover up my frozen nothingness
With a warm blanket of deep thought and know
That, tho' I had no hearth thro' years, I bless
Still in thy gift a hearth known long ago.

I seek it ever in my friends and dream
Of its rich fire that went so darkly out
So everlastingly. Nothing doth seem
As sure to me again. I halt. I doubt

With icy ponderings upon this bank
Far on downriver from that house once glad
With book, and bread, and music, and I thank
Thee for some love perhaps I have not had.

Why is this tremulous thing so needful that
I yet would count it the sole star of night
To lead me out of marshes, flat
And dim detours to come unto the light

Of ultimate mountains? O I do not know
What loss I had within the soul that set
Me so afraid, unsure, but still I go
Looking for love within the darkness yet.

5th October 1971

## A Sleeper in a Sea-Port Town

O thou night wind, I heard thee constantly
Within my keyhole and I shrank and crept,
When I was twenty, late to bed and slept
Thro' the void hours a deeper sleep for thee,

Because within my dreamless plane I knew
In some hid vestige of the mind thou went
Abroad in that sea town, by chimneys, spent
Against shut doors, and everlasting blew

An elegy of skerries not on maps,
Never on earth, and for my rest I had
Within my consciousness two worlds, one sad,
Haunted and old, and one more loved perhaps

Because while thou, cloud-bearded, still did'st play
Above my sleep, my sleep I knew to grow
Warm and more safe. As violets under snow
My thoughts hid, thankful, to the break of day.

9th October 1971


## To an unknown ancestor, maybe

They do come dropping down to me
On thin threads of eternity,
My songs,
And all that unto them belongs;

And who wrote first, that these words come
(Or they come not, and I am dumb,
But start
At some wild star that lights the heart),

I know not, but as dawn unlocks
The night's old shadowy music box
I seize
A pen as struck by destinies

Far beyond anything I know
Born out of sight ages ago
By some
Chanceling from whose blood I come;

And how did the first rapture light
Upon that maker in his night?
Did he
Know my exact felicity?

What thou did'st then, old miscreant, thou
Hast much to claim or disavow
Alack!
I bear thy soul upon my back.

10th October 1971


## The Locked Door


Through all the dark fields of absence
I love you yet.
In the mazed lanes of all the nights
I never forget
The terrible vacuity in which
This twenty years your star is set.

O life, how shall I ever
Open that door
Remembered on that final room
The air haggard and hoar
Where he had dwelt to hear my footsteps climb
Patient, bright-eyed, through years before?

O friend of whom I never speak
Some stratum deep
Below my merry earthly heart
That room doth keep
With all its hopes and peace and pain untouched
Until with you at last I sleep.

There is no blessing for us two ever
Than the night.
Nothing will serve us more in this world.
I stoop and write
Some trivial words until eternity
Crawls on the dial into sight.

That I could go to sleep and waken
Never, never!
That you could come on the dawn wind!
For ever, for ever.
To turn from these cold ruinous stars and come,
Thankful, all done, past that locked room.

                                    31st October 1971

# If I forget thee

*For Father Alexander Burgess*

If I forget thee it is not because
I love thee less but in thy love I know
Such rest as lets me hesitate and pause
By the new sights that thy own worth did show
Unto my mind that formerly did see
But half a landscape when it knew not thee.

If I delay, it is the holy course
That thou did'st set that takes me from thy side
By marvellous isles and havens, thee the source
Of freedoms that must yet our lives divide
Ev'n while they join them. If 'twere otherwise
We should have nought but love's infirmities.

14th November 1971

# To one who sleeps by night and day

Hast thou such wastes within that thou must sleep
To dull the raindrop on the window pane
Lest thy life, hearing it, should stir and weep
For all the things thou did'st exclude in vain,

The rare, the painted hour, the exquisite
On which thou turned'st thy back and still did'st sneer
That these were but vain myths? The morning's light
Died in thy want as in a sepulchre.

All, all things thou did'st need, because thou wert
The neediest heart that trod these highways yet,
Lopped from all chances and kept close, inert,
By the dark tie within thy brain long set

That must thee hinder from each earthly love,
Each warm and tender margin that might touch
Another's life. Thou thought'st thyself above,
Who wert below, and now hast but a crutch

Of desperate sleep to lean on, so that thou
Can'st shut the thronging camp out evermore,
But, fearing still an echo in thy brow
Arise, take opiates, lock a darker door.

26th November 1971


## Remembering a Child's Christmas Eve

If I should grow so weary I
None of the famous spring espy
Within the snowflake passing by

Let this poor body turn to be
Snowflakes, hummocks, century,
Part of this beauty I now see.

O let me not outlive the time
When a hill pony still will climb
To share my supper in the rime,

And I can through the silence feel
Its homely satisfaction steal
As its white breath above our meal.

I would ask nothing more than this.
No heavenly garden, curious bliss,
But the rough earth's own chance-won kiss

And that thin faculty that doth go
To find delight in furzes low
On Christmas Eve ere the first snow.

1st December 1971


## The Dipper's Nest that Overhangs
## the River

Pass by most quietly this quiet nest
But keep it like a jewel in thy breast.
It and its bright inhabitant will save
Thee from some grave.

Her care, her watchful silence will stay nigh
To comfort thee when thirty years go by.
Thou shalt take strength amid some deadly strife
From this hid life.

There is some vestige of divinity
Fast plaited here upon a long-branched tree
Above a stream. Some hour this nest will come
To seem thy home,

And thou shalt turn to it as tho' thou wert
The very occupant, silent, alert,
And this long-finished dome be to thy heart
Armour and art.

2nd December 1971

# The Tramp

Alas for Lazarus who doth go
Wadded without, and cloaked in snow,
The bread in his torn pocket damp,
His destination a dim lamp
Across three fields where he may find
A can of tea to light his mind.

What does he think of? Nought; the night,
Dumb and inured unto his plight.
Such a brave silence comes from far
Journeying below his faithless star.
Should he gain nothing at that door
He will go on, cross three fields more.

Such a dark energy sets in this
Poor vagabond in place of bliss.
Reft of all comfort still he knows
Thro' endless searches, roofed with snows,
Some seed of hope. He will not die,
But trudges on, he knows not why.

Give him tonight a bed of hay,
He has great riches until day
Break on the lasting fields and he
Again an empty man will be,
Yet in his emptiness have some
Ghost-built indomitable home.

3rd December 1971

## Sleep on Canisp, Sutherland

Afar in the dark, dark Canisp keeps
The margins of a thousand sleeps
Pent in her rocks. A thousand eyes
Are shuttered with tranquillities.
Blow, rise, storm winds, rove
No membrane stirs in all I love.

All ye great rocks darken and flood
With deeper hues the sleep of the blood.
Make the soft pulse to beat more slow
In breast and head. The loud winds blow
Forests of sleep to shelter them
Who nothing utter by root and stem.

3rd December 1971


## The Solitaries

The merry badger keeps his way
Nocturnally,
And I go merry to my play
Even as he.

Minding our own business
Tending our own,
We are no more than this.
Leave us alone.

1971

167

# To my Manuscripts

Shall I take ye with me
From the world
Shall I bury both of us,
Your pages curled
By the kitchen flame while I
Haste silently

Unto my home to grow
Nothing again?
I would not leave ye here to speak
Of our long vain
Struggles in tempests set
But spare ye yet.

Ye are my echoing heart.
I see in ye
Nothing I set out with
Or planned to be,
But the poor wraiths that dance
By circumstance.

I should take ye with me
When I die
That we go to bed at last
Both quietly
Lapped in our dusks, no more
Than packman's lore.

'Twould be our perfect word
To end as one
That colloquy which we know
Best unbegun.
Why do I hesitate?
The night is late.

4th December 1971

## On a Child's Company

Here, succoured by his fancies grim
Or lovely, plays a child. On him
Take mercy that he comes to thee
As to his inn most naturally

And whil'st thou sayest nought, tells all
His lurid, innocent wish. But fall
With agitation to thy knee
And forcèd sense, then utterly

Thou shalt have lost the pure account,
The centre of the vision mount
Past thy shut heart, and thou shalt be
Poorer by a whole treasury.

Think not to love him. Only wait
Casual to appreciate
All that this little child may know
And thou shalt see the gods below.

5th December 1971


## I would not leave thee

I would not leave thee to the echoing night.
Bewilderment, writhed dreams, but thou hast made
Somehow a coppice for thy soul. The bright
And exquisite stars look down and are afraid

For thy young hours that are so twisted now
With strange affliction, but I love thee still
As when thou wert the singer on my bough
As when thou wert the daylight on my hill.

I cannot salve by one small art, nor know
How in this world to knit thy sense again
But turn unto my road and silent go
'Til memory be all that lights my brain.

Yet why thou didst this thing, where'er I tread
I still must ask sometimes. The moon, the wind
Have yet their periods, Thou seemst with the dead
Fixèd, like them, unchang'd, for ever blind.

O take one step, one glimpse. Thy glorious youth
Waits still upon the threshold. I would turn,
Retrace my steps, and take thee still by smooth
And common paths where all the foothills burn

With fortunate summer that for thee did rise
Out of a winter night like thine, and waits
Crowned with her gentle flowers to greet thine eyes
If thou wilt raise them to the dawn's white gates.

6th December 1971

## To a Friend, Grown Apart
## Through Circumstances

Thou took'st the cascade from the mountain
Thou took'st the windflower from the plain
But I will never ask of thee
'Bring these again',

For I know no joy got from asking.
For me all is in vain
And when thou com'st to count thy prize
Nought will remain.

Thou hast lost, even as I, the vision,
The stream will darken with winter's rain.
The flower did not grow for one heart
But for us twain.

10th December 1971


## Remembering the Sleep I had in Gedna-grain, in the West of Sutherland

Come to me now, bright winds of sleep.
Take me to dwell
Beyond all shores, beyond the mind's own deep
Dark-searching bell
That too oft for me tolls,
Bringing figments of souls

I loved not in any land,
Relinquish now
And by your muffled, guarded verges stand,
Nothing avow
To take from here but look
Within a cloud-filled book.

Let no white page be writ upon.
As when a child
Loses itself in vision, let me be gone,
Pastured, beguiled,
Miles past experience.
Let me be herded hence.

11th December 1971

## Remembering the Mersey, 1941

Dark are thy waters, O Mersey,
Yet they did bud with fire,
And thus do I remember thee
And my sunk youth's desire
To live one night more, to see again
The quays, the ruins, the falling rain.

Thou took'st my life, thou suffering river,
That I will never be
What I was before or ever
Forget thy passion and thee,
Or the night watch, the buried art,
The buried childhood in my heart.

Flames, torment, the sleepless time
Have long since gone by,
And from these did my senses climb
Into a serer sky.
Years do not part us nor eclipse
The valour of thy murdered ships.

6th January 1972


## To Ships that never came home

O all ye ships, who never did come back,
A northland of proud silent hearts is here
To be your fire, who must all firesides lack,
Knowing but the grey foam that is your bier,

Who never shall hear stalwart children more
Bless ye with joy through any harbour gate,
Nor see the welcoming faces on the shore.
We are the last shreds of your earthly fate,

And we shall keep with ye forever, still
The pictures of old love graved in our heart;
The sea-wharf walk, the tryst upon the hill,
The marriage morn, the dancing ever start

In our dark consciousness that doth ye hold
Always from the cross-tide, the ruining sea.
Hid in some house of time is all your gold
To spend in lives that do remember ye.

19th January 1972


## In a Scots Express

Cocooned in a train,
Neither here nor there,
I have left last night
Last night's despair.

I have not yet come
To tomorrow's care,
Rapt out of time
With life set fair.

Wheels turn on
To put me somewhere,
But tonight is tonight
I am out of the snare.

God bless all trains
That keep such rare
Galaxies, chasms
'Twixt here and there.

2nd February 1972

## An Unearned Blessing

This is my caesura of the night
This is my midnight
In which I remember not the past
Nor dream of any future light
But keep this moment while it last.

This is my pause betwixt life and life
This is my true life.
It will not stay but will soon buried be
By vagueries the packs of strife
Tomorrow's winds that wait for me.

O silent hour held high above hope
Better than all hope
How art thou blest, sustained when thou dost come
A height past thought, instincts that grope
To hold me chained in this low room.

I am no man's poor prisoner now
In my eventual now
Nothing portends that happened e'er before
Freedom from earth's desires, no vow
Can bring thee ever to my door.

This is my caesura of the night.
This is my midnight.
Farewell, my visitor, thou wilt soon be gone.
I do but thank thee for respite
Knowing thou wilt return anon.

4th February 1972

## On going through the dormitory of a mental hospital at night

Poor, patient, laid in layers, I pity ye
As thro' your dusky dormitory I go
And none with angry words doth question me
When I pass nightly by your beds, altho'

The door rasps on its jamb. Like to the dead
Ye lie in thankfulness for rest, and then
I love ye for your protest never said
And for your buried dreams, half-risen again.

All succoured, hidden from bewilderment
In your crouched pillows as I pass ye by
Each keeps alone some figment of content
Tho' outside wheels the storm's dark heraldry.

Ours is one fate within this levelling hour.
Some fast wood of the night doth us engross,
And bends and housels all things in its power,
And never do our verges come more close.

8th February 1972

## On the dark side of poetry

Thou bring'st a sombre stuff with thee
O poetry.
Thou bring'st where bright stars glow
Great steeps of snow.
Voids and cold seas where no ships dare to tread
Are still thy bed.

Yet this poor art, riven and caught
By thee, counts naught
The pauper's candle, rain
On rag-stuffed pane,
The clambering shadows on the damp-hued wall
For thou art all.

February 1972

## To Alice

Alice, when thou did'st wed my kin
Thou should'st have had great claws and teeth,
A very serpent's acumen
To hold such basilisks beneath,

And I should have been born divine,
Omniscient, watchful night and day,
But God be praised that kin decline
And sometimes mice get out to play.

2nd June 1972

## Voyage of a Ship
### A Childhood Memory

I watched this wood when I was five years old
And thought it was a ship and that it went
Unto Australia, sea-trunks in its hold
And every morning for six weeks I spent

Counting its stages on its far-off hill
To the Antipodes. I never knew
Its sea was snow-wreaths, that the north wind still,
That seemed to speed it unto Melbourne, blew

Among strained pines and rutted rocks. I saw
How it had scarcely moved since yesterday.
Yet I believed it moved by its own law,
And watched that it kept safely on its way;

And then I heard the ship I thought it was,
The 'Medic', had reached port through storms and ills,
But, visible yet, the wood ne'er gave me pause.
Melbourne, I saw, was in the Cawdor hills.

4th June 1972


## Envoi

Beneath this innocent plain that was your soul
You kept a dark root that I never knew,
And slowly from its deep place it grew whole
To a scarce-comprehended, poisonous yew.

177

So I will never seek that plain again,
Mistrust its summer and its flowers that grow
Maybe close by that root that brought me pain
And withers all things that we once did know.

25th June 1972

## On a Process of Remembering

When I fix in the forepart of my brain
Something I want to seep the after part
Tables and kitchen chairs stand out most plain
Around me, tho' I know not by what art
I order images to come again,

Forgot thro' many days, to stir and wake
At their right moment from the buried past
Yet at their true hour they will shine and take,
Like an alarm, darkness to day at last,
And keep their lists, disorder order make.

I should go farther, find how all this mark
That grows a ghost is raised alive, anew,
When I do lay with foresight in the dark
And common things stand plain, what is't I do?
I know some compass that brings home my barque.

9th July 1972

## On meeting a solitary woman reading in the basin-room of a mental hospital

A wan and unloved figure meets me here,
Brown-clad, and she is one the same as I,
For, though I may have jewels in the sky
On earth I am a sober passenger.

This never-speaking woman reaches to
Deep artery and heart and finds them bare,
Vagrant as she, dark fearful chambers where
The dawn breaks never and the winds blow through.

O sounding wind, some time blow hope and grace
Ev'n in such deserts. Surely there must be
On earth some ray of light, some certainty
To cure the wraiths within this hapless place.

                                        28th July 1972


## On a stained-glass window of Our Lady

This is the Virgin's shrine. The bright beams come
Down from her womb where the Lord Jesus stands
Radiant, a babe within his too-short home.
And even there He has transfixed hands.

                                        2nd August 1972

## The Passing of Beauty

All beautiful things fall from the air
In dust and moulted feathers.
Long ago my swan went where
Some other river tethers
Hope and pageant and light
With loops of night.

Long ago my goldfinch flew
To its last thistle and fell,
Younger than day or dew,
Straight to the fields of hell.
My life grows less and less.
Comes nothingness.

undated

## That we have no angels

What do I weep for? That we have no angels,
The hunted otter, and the fox, and I.
We are expendible. No dream, no pain tells
To any heart our dark extremity.

We are alone. On byroads and wan river
No ghost of mercy watches us and we
Fall from the day, my little kin, as never
Upon the earth had we been born to be.

Enjoy this hour only, my bright-eyed otter.
O my red fox, from thy high hillside see
In peace thy fellow in his spherèd water
And one sole human who loves him and thee.

This afternoon the price of all the darkness
Pays to our souls. Take it. The wind is free,
The stream. If there were angels none could mark less
Than that we lived, reached our identity.

18th October 1972

## To a Siskin

Thou, little siskin, still did'st know
To make thy nest in fir-trees low,
Yet with their tender branches cleft
To hold thy work, hidden and deft.

How shall I, who have lost thy art,
Nor found a better one, e'er start
To build with my superior mind
As good a hospice from the wind?

Thou art a poem of life. For me,
I do but write my poetry
With shreds and cantos grasped from some
Brain half-articulate, half-dumb;

And thou shalt leave this nest to go
Afield, even as I, but know
That thou hast left, forgot, behind
An instance of a perfect mind.

7th November 1972

# The River

Love was a river found out the wrong ocean.
It travelled there with all its jewels and songs
By many shadows, suns. With calm emotion
It ran into the sea, but naught belongs

Of all its secrets there. It has found never
A fate that fillèd its sweet course but came
Only to discords, reefs. Unhappy river
That now does its own . . . wanderings blame.

Were its jewels false, its waterfalls hoarse thunder
Or was its sea not worth the reaching? O
In threaded streams, unwelcoming pools, its wonder
Finished at last does now in darkness go.

21st November 1972


# An Old Purse

Out of you came many deeds,
Books, and bright days, a stony crown.
Oft-strained poor host of all my needs,
The cobbled street, the scarlet gown
Never were born but for you
Whom unpraised labours filled anew.
Tattered as I, within this north-east town
As a saint's relic yet I lay you down.

9th December 1972

# To a Dog

*'Be you faithful unto death and I will give you a crown of life.'*

A crown of life upon that humble head
Prize of fidelity, men did not see,
But it will shine when all my words are said,
When both of us are dust and centaury.

O friend of shadows, journeys, lonesome streets,
Echoes, and hunger, there was none like thee.
Until the dogstar with the daystar meets
Gay-pawed, brave-hearted, thou go'st still with me.

18th December 1972

# A Shelf of Books

When I was young the gold was in me.
The merry streams were in my blood.
When the sun gleamed on some corporeal river
Myself it was in flood

On to more gold, to more horizons.
Now the sweet gilding of a book
That was my friend in youth calls back the river
If I but stand and look.

My friends are firm among the shadows.
I cannot lose, tho' I grow old,
The pleading star, the innate word of mosses.
O the unchangèd gold!

1972

## To a Fellow Patient (L. Cooper)

Ev'n in the grey clouds of thy being
Thou hast the kindness to remember me
And when I walk apart, deprived, unseeing
Thou comest silently
To put some trivial gift within my hand
And I, renewed, travel a brighter land.

15th April 1973

## On the virtue of a single meeting

O meet me once, I am the stranger
Bent steeply on the earthly road;
But meet me twice, thou see'st the danger
Of lightening my load.

'Maybe this stranger has forgotten
To sign the cheque and pay the fief!
Maybe his heart is mildewed, rotten,
A pariah, a thief!'

So meet me once, my friend, with smiling
Like the fair morning in thy face,
And then forget me, yet beguiling
My whole life with thy grace.

1st June 1973

# Desperate for love

Desperate for love one winter night
I walked the streets to see it burst
Like the meridian or a comet's light
Upon this heart so cursed.

Everywhere was the wall-cold face.
The wrapped and hurrying forms went by,
And I returned with slow steps to my place
Longing to sleep or die.

We are such towers of flesh I think
No ray of joy can fly between
Our dark shot windows and our souls do shrink
To husks mere, parchèd, mean.

Desperate for love one winter night
I walked the streets to see it bloom
Like the fair Virgin on my starvèd sight
But I came hungry home.

16th June 1973

# Hostess without Guests

Lost in this desert hospital
Without a single cat to fall
In folds about my feet, or see
A speculative dog watch me

With brown eyes that ne'er quarrel but
Look on me as an equal put
Here to dispense toast, gossip, tea,
My God, what will become of me?

22nd June 1973

## To Nurse Hoare's Father

Though thou long to bed art gone
Rest thy living eyes upon
The sole mountain, the sere star
'Til it comes, afar, afar,

From its height to dwell with thee
Silently, insensately
To its low home in thy breast
There to give thee sleep and rest.

1973

## A Landscape Remembered

For miles each wood, each pasture you have caught
By your clear brush that knew entirety
And the proud lowering sky. I have forgot
Your name, but evermore your thought I see,

A country where my loosened heart can pierce
'Tho I stir never from this fireside chair,
And tho' the winter's wind blow soft or fierce
I stand, most blest, among the stubbles there.

7th July 1973

# To the Soul

Hast thou gone to sleep, my beloved?
Do the moats and doors of memory shut thee out?
Does temporal joy exclude thee from our marriage,
The minstrels' music frighten thee?

Nay, I go down the dark stairway
Of the mind, alone, without music or torches
Or remembered joys or figures or mountain dances,
Or the dreams in a wrought wine-cup.

I bear nothing, since nothing thou needest
Or can ever need, alone, untriumphing,
Perfect amid the dusks of thy small chamber
That is the vergeless universe.

Neither young nor old, my beloved,
Older than the stars, younger than dew,
Thou keepest, hid. I leave the mortal dancing
To stay always alone with thee.

1st September 1973

## I have the past, the green lands

I have the past, the green lands
Tonight as ne'er before.
Thou need'st not close the curtains,
Nor lock and bar the door,

For this land comes by courses
I know not, nor is lost
By chances nor by dangers
That has five bridges crossed

Of the five rich-born senses
That keep each moment whole.
Thou need'st not close the curtains
That curtain not the soul.

9th July 1973

*The Last Years*
*1974–1976*

## This is my land

This is my land you cannot touch,
It is the land beyond the vein
Beyond the rooted hair, so much
Lies here that may not show again

Its form upon the earthly day
But yet in twenty years may rise
Out of the cells of being to play
Child-like, one hour beneath the skies,

Then never more. Trysted unto
The labyrinth that brought it forth
It mixes with its peers again
Secure from chains of wealth or worth.

8th February 1974


## I have such joy

I have such joy to be alive
I am so happy to feel well.
All the sorrows lie outside
All the heavenly roses dwell

In this blest now which like a star
Of holy Cygnus lights my way.
I am more rich than princes are
That I know this one day.

30th March 1974

# A Thanksgiving to the Holy Ghost

Holy Ghost, to you I pray
To you I did escape away
From frustrate heart and poverty
With my black dog beside my knee.

You kept other streets to bless,
Unjudging, want and weariness—
Other poverties maybe
But not the one that handcuffed me.

Holy Ghost your light I thank
That lights the violet on the bank
The things I had no will to see
The wild thrush on his apple tree.

Tho' I have want and pain and need
I bear you here, a secret seed
And as the thrush, the seed, am free
In a great world that welcomes me.

9th May 1974


# What is this need of love?

What is this need of love that we have made
Immense cathedrals for a being to dwell
To love us in? There we have knelt and prayed
For love        When the Sanctus bell

Pealed at the altar, we have thought we knew
That love to come, a shining river nigh
Our poor spent hearts, and yet it was our own
Dearth and desire that brought eternity,

A false eternity, still only time,
To smooth our thoughts, make the unbearable
Yet to be borne. 'Tis we ourselves who climb
Up, up, to what? By what imagined hill?

We were not loved within our cradles, peers,
Nor in our childhood, seven parts forlorn,
Begot without a dream. Yet instincts fierce
Unquenchable, rage to create some morn

Of love, better than this, better than all.
Humble I stand to see such feeling go
About the earth, nor know what may befall
From our humanity, what tower may grow.

12th May 1974


## To my Mother

You called me evil, and I grew
To think that I was evil too.
No gift I gave you but it proved
Unlov'd. And yet the stars I loved,

The green tree and the quaking brake,
And to these hospices I take
My soul. Yet what you sowed runs stark
Like a hell's river in the dark:

And sometimes here I think it will
Drown the green tree, the saving hill.
Nothing I do on earth is fair,
For I am she should not be there.

How did you hate a babe that had
Nothing but innocence and glad
Reaching towards the future. This
Riddle of birth is my abyss.

I would have brought you all the land,
Skylarks, the fishes on the strand,
The very sun. But you did say
'Evil, depart and stay away.'

24th June 1974


## Nobody will come

Nobody will come, my love,
In the winter's rain.
In the dingy-sheeted bed
Turn to me again
Lie we close in silence bound
'Til we both are underground.
Nobody will come tonight.
Nobody will ever
Step below the church's wall,
Cross the flying river
To separate yourself and me
Desperate faithful poverty.

3rd August 1974

*To* —— ——

Your name was charity. You gave, and took
My love and hope and all away.
Now I must write down in a darkened book
Charity like an ass did bray.

3rd August 1974

*Dreamed 2nd January 1975:
midnight low mass in a Jesuit church*

Here's the star of morn unfled
   *Zou mow sas agape.*
Here's the light of the world to silence wed,
   My Life, I love Thee.

2nd January 1975

*On a Picture of a Gold-Haired
Child Riding*

Once I was you, I rode like you
On your small pony through the night.
My coat was fur and cherry hue
Like yours, and I was decked in light

As you. But then I saw you were
The past, the loved, the guarded thing,
And I know now the winters where
The snows fall and the hail will sting

And yet tonight you are again
Myself, o happy child, and I
Bless this bright minute far from pain,
Blossom of the soul's mystery.

Ride on, red-coated, through the gloom
Unto some house of joy I knew
And I will catch your rein and come
Furred, safe, rich-coated, loved like you.

23rd January 1975


## The Owl

O you pure owl
Who call within the night,
Speaking with thoughts inborn of the night,
How you do melt away
The day and its decay.

When I walk to your tree
I walk through aisles of night,
The clustered glooms and shards of night,
And underneath you I
Am born again, or die.

You care not, blessed one.
You care not tho' I watch
Any more than the million stars that watch
Me in the night care aught.
In this uncaring I grow naught;

Not as by daylight when I am
The feeble spectacle.
Now I am calm and no man's spectacle.
The scarecrow blood that should have died
Walks with owl-splendid glooms inside.

1975

## For lack of love

For lack of love I have a star
An owl, a stream-side nenuphar,
And these will do me all my days
And these alone my heart will praise

17th January 1976

## Long Ago

Long ago when I was loved
Love was like a winter cloak
Love was like a sheltering oak
   O long ago.

Every forest had its bird
Every flower spoke to me,
Every bird cried hopefully
   O long ago.

But the cloak was rent in two
And the oak the lightning slew
Cold the wind cried and blew
   O long ago.

Now sweet love I importune.
Answer only star and moon
The grebe and the uncaring loon,
   O long ago!

18th January 1976

## The Dream Castle

When I came to a drawbridge light
I crossed the drawbridge and came to
The castle of the inner sight,
Where all the long dark hours through
I walked with thoughts I never knew.

I never knew myself before
Nor know myself when I awake,
But know behind the ghostly door
Of that strange castle that I make
Mysteries, poems that will not take

Flight when the day is in its power
And castle, drawbridge, all are gone.
Yet in my veins through every hour
My deep-laid home still lingers on,
Will light some sun has not yet shone.

by 25th May 1976

## Sanctuary—The Kootenay Ram

I think of the faraway Kootenay ram.
I think of lonesome places.
When you speak to me with unkindly words
I think of sheeps' faces
Grazing the untrod grasses.
I think of high passes.

Far, far up beyond envy and scorn
I see a grey trout rising
From his fast stream. Tho' I am patched and rent
This is my disguising
Forced on my flesh—I know it.
My sun shines below it;

Shining on the hazed mountains yet
Where you will never see
The peace, the dawns, the whimbrels that were made
For my soul's almonry.
Against your ravening words
I hear the foothill birds.

1976

## A Sleepless Dawn

My tiredness will show through
Even a verse on dew.
My sickness will be seen
Altering all things I mean

Into a feverish bed
Tossed by a restless head
So I had better keep
Nothing but silence—sleep.

30th May 1976

## Me a poor dying rotten thing

Me a poor dying rotten thing
Unto some bliss of creatures bring
That I shall not for ever be lone
But come at last unto my own

Whether it be by trusting nest
Or friend's words that I am blest.
O home that I long look to see
I am foredone for want of thee.

1976

## Reach for Andromeda

Reach for Andromeda, because you can,
And if you can, you can reach higher far,
For least and highest live within a man,
The darker suborner and the brightest star,
And gods and criminals entangled are
Within our veins. O how do we descry
The worm, the vernal star, the low, the high!

Reach for Andromeda and if you may
Come not unto that alien galaxy,
You shall at least reach to some purest day
That yet will bathe and strengthen ardently
Your life and all sweet common things that be
Under, within, around your heart and have
That happiness that all your life will save.

Reach for Andromeda, though nights are dark
With sullen senses. Reach on high unto
The world outside the world. A golden spark
Of heaven will light up all this world and you.
Never sink by the lane-side. Lo! a hue
Not of this earth does still surround you now.
Still in the dark I strive and know not how.

I know not why my nerves and veins and blood
Long for the infinite, and know not why
Butterfly's wing, and cumulus, and flood
Take me, a spirit, to the highest sky
Where no dusked thought or memory comes by.
Only I know beyond all human ken
My soul touches Andromeda again.

3rd September 1976

# On Meeting Twentysix Swans in a River

None offers me fight
  All pass me by
On a hundred little currents,
  Twixt riverbed and sky.
Though all must see my boat
  All mind their own,
Crossing like me above
  Shallow and stone.

O love in this Welsh river
  Love that takes no part
O'er these long years I thank you
  Out of my heart.
This night I remember
  Purposes, rivulets,
Your paths, our morning journey
  Nothing of me forgets.

7th September 1976

# Notes

p.47 *Biviers*: Olive had spent that summer vacation working in France.

p.51 *Fugue of Morning*: *quo fugit venator, per silvam, per vitam?* —'which way does the hunter speed, both pursuing and being pursued, through the wood, through life'. Olive would not divulge the source of this epigraph, nor has it been traced.

p.53 *Apple land*: Just before graduation and the end of student days some of the group of friends gathered in the home of Jean B. W. Sinclair. Present were Davidina Bonner (later Mrs Garden), Lesley Chalmers, Helen Stevens, Norah Sinclair (a younger sister) and Olive. The poem read aloud set them arguing 'who was which?' and Jean declared she had been left out. So Olive added lines specifically for her.

p.55 *The Vikings*: Sulna-stapa and Herlesferd: Olive would never tell why these particular placenames were chosen.

p.56 *A Nocturnal to Poetry*: Olive mis-spells 'satyrion', the orchis, as 'satyrian'.

p.57 *Envoi to Poetry*: a variant from an undated text is in *The Pure Account*. Other variants and drafts exist.

WAR AND AFTER WAR 1940–1949

p.62 *To Poetry*: written in St Francis Hospital, East Dulwich, a mental hospital, later merged in the hospital nexus with Bexley Hospital. Olive could have been briefly in St Francis Hospital during her later spells of treatment at Bexley Hospital (1956–61). But it appears likely that she was in hospital after the termination of her service in the WRNS.

p.62 *Pastoral*: The *curriculum vitae* she prepared for the Bodleian Library Committee mentions the flock of Rhode Island

Reds she raised while doing landwork in her home area, 1942–44.

p.63 *On a Distant Prospect*: Stanzas 7–12 are absent from one version, stanzas 11–12 from two others.

p.66 *V.E. Day 1945*: thrang/ thronging; won awa' frae/ got away from; ilka/ each, every; ditty/ 1) song 2) obligation, undertaking; laverock/ lark.

p.66 *Victory Ode*: Breendonck was an SS torture camp in Belgium; 'a cobbled port'/ Nairn; 'an ancient stony crown'/ the crown-tower of King's College, Old Aberdeen. Of the world-war triumvirate, Roosevelt was dead; of the family microcosm of three women, the beloved great-aunt had died in 1944.

p.70 *The King's Student*: a variant is in *The Pure Account*. Callimachus (310–c.240 B.C.), a learned poet and playwright, was the librarian of the royal library at Alexandria. The two colleges of Aberdeen University are King's, a medieval foundation, and Marischal, a reformation college.

p.70 *To a ship*: Skidbladnir—Olive mistakenly took this to be the name of a ship of Odin, a 'ship of the dead'. See her poem 'The Eve of St Mark'.

p.71 *On a stoned and dying Cygnet*: there are many variants of this poem's title. Olive appears to be conscious, yet unwilling to say openly that it is not unknown for a cygnet to be killed by the male parent—and the dying bird to be thereafter stoned by human kind. Did she see a parallel to her own lot?

p.74 *The Mountain Bird* or *The Dipper*: Leslie Sutherland was the first war casualty at sea of 'the children of Nairn' who had been Olive's childhood playmates. The dipper is the Water Ousel, *cinclus aquaticus* (because it 'plays' in the water); Fearna (Fiarna) 'the river of the alders' according to Olive, —the River Nairn.

p.77 *Within this little testament*: Herb Trinity is viola tricolor, the pansy or heartsease, 'for remembrance'.

p.78 *In a Glen Garden*: the poem 'Afar in the bright sun' has many drafts and its entitling varies in the first element, now 'In a Hill Garden . . .', now 'In a Glen Garden . . .'. The second of these has been chosen here, to distinguish this from the poem that follows 'Thee thou old Syrian man' which is consistently entitled 'In a Hill Garden'. Stanza 6: the blitz on Merseyside included a direct hit on a maternity hospital.

p.85 *A cold night on Croome's Hill*: In Greenwich, the Ursuline Convent there has a statue of Jesus in its garden, visible to the passer-by. Olive spells the name 'Croome's Hill' throughout her writings. The title is once extended '. . . London), near the Church of Our Lady, Star of the Sea'.

p.86 *The Visionary Land* or *The Poet (I)*: Dunedin is Edinburgh. Duntulm, an ancient fortress of the Macdonalds on the west coast of Scotland; Thebes because there the conquering Alexander, while wasting the city, spared the house that had been Pindar's, as Milton recalls in his sonnet that he had pinned on his own door 'When the assault was intended to the city' (Sonnet VIII: 'Captain, or colonel, or knight at arms,').

p.86 *On an old woman*: Anthea is one of several names used in her poetry for Miss Ann Maria Jeans, the beloved great-aunt who brought her up.

p.89 *Written in London*: 'A lost poem remembered in a dream, 1.15am August 27, 1976, 26 years after composition.'

p.89 *Meadow Rain*: Loch Ewe is the name of both loch and adjacent peak.

p.90 *Requiem for Dives*: Dives as in Dives and Lazarus, (Luke, Ch.16); probably written for William McDougall, well-to-do merchant in Aberdeen, (husband of her father's sister Elizabeth Fraser) whose conduct was not propitious to the fortunes of Olive, her mother or her greataunt Jeans. Gloss: routh/ plentifully supplied; lyart/ streaked with grey and white (as in granite); wynds/ narrow lanes in a town.

p.91 *Harpsong for Alban*: Olive working from memory, using older maps and earlier scholarship, says 'Alban' for Scotland, not 'Alba'. Her spelling of Gaelic words can be antiquated or mistaken. Correct spelling is now supplied or an acceptable version in English (names within brackets are from current maps). Clarsach/ the small Celtic harp; Beinn a Choirein—the hill of the little corrie (there is a 'Beinn a Chaoruinn' NE of Ben Macdhui in SW Banffshire); Beinn a' Ghlo—in Perthshire, NE of Blair Atholl; Glen na h-Alban/ Glen of Scotland; Glen Geoullie—west bank of the Spey south of Knockando; Caiplich—beyond Tomintoul; Eaglais Choluim/ church of Columba (there are several).

p.92 *The Eagle to his Children*: Gleann na h'Iolaire/ glen of the eagle;

Gleann a Chruitire/ glen of the harper; Gleannan Fada/ the long little glen; Hallival (Haleval) in Rhum or Healabhal (Healaval Mor and Beg/ big and little) in Skye, flat-topped eminences known as 'MacLeod's Tables': these last were formerly believed to have been sites of pagan veneration. Olive, with earlier scholars, discerned a 'holy' element in the name, but some say it means flagstone fell. *Agnus dei*—O lamb of God: invocation in the Mass; Clan Ranald/ the Macdonalds; Clan Alpin/ probably the Macgregors; Clan Sim/ a branch of the Frasers. Olive had relatives named MacDonald and McGregor.

p.94 *The Eve of St Mark*: the author glosses: 'machair/ a meadow by the sea, pronounced with "a" as in bank, "ch" as in loch; mor, Gaelic for "big" pronounced "more", one of the commonest epithets in a country where all the members of a family may have the same Christian name'. Torquil is Scandinavian Thorkil gaelicised, a man's forename. *Miserere Domine,* Be merciful, O Lord.

p.97 *Benighted in the Cairngorms*: several versions have 'to' for 'in'; Author's gloss: 'mawkin/ hare; cranreuch/ hoar-frost; the nicht/ tonight; A'an/ Ben Avon; lift/ sky; ava/ at all; lums/ chimneys; smeek/ smoke'. Author's note: 'Alnack—both stream and crag, beyond Tomintoul, pronounced Alnyack; Caiplich—both stream and crag beyond Tomintoul pronounced Kyplich'. Gloss: meat/ food; fit/ foot; troot/ trout; hern/ heron. Note—line 6 'herd' is in some versions 'head'.

p.98 *The Glen of the Clearance*: one of the prize-winning poems of 1951. The text as subsequently printed in *The Mercat Cross,* Vol.4, (1952), pp.148–9 has several differences in punctuation and capitalisation, e.g. Mass/ mass—and these different readings: st.3 smileth/ shineth; st.9 Clann Fhearguis/ Clan Domnuill; st.11 Clan Sim/ Clan of Sim; st.14 of Fhearguis/ of Domnuill. While Clan of Sim or of Fergus would be branches of the Frasers, Clan of Domnuill appears to draw into the poem's concern the Macdonalds of the Glencoe massacre, a further echo of suffering. (She had MacDonald kin on her mother's side.) The names should read 'Clann Domhnaill' and 'children of Domhnall'. The printed text glosses whimbrel/curlew, bield/shelter, eyas/young hawk. The version given here is from a typescript, prepared certainly later than 1952. The meaning and the context of the macaronic 'refrain lines' are as follows, stanza by stanza:

1—'Thou shall sprinkle me'—This is said before High Mass.

2—'And my cry shall come unto Thee'—part of the Ordinary of the Mass, said at the foot of the altar, after the confession of sins.

3—'Lord hear our cry'; from a psalm set for mass on one day in Holy Week.

4 & 5, in order, 'Lord have mercy upon us'; 'Glory to God in the highest'. [Collect, Epistle, Gradual . . . Gospel . . .]

6—'and life everlasting'—at the end of the Creed.

7—'when we remember Thee, O Zion' from a psalm set for mass on one day in Holy Week.

8—'an evening sacrifice'—Offertory of High Mass, the blessing of the incense.

9—'the flame of (Thine) eternal love'—the blessing of the thurible, of fire.

10—'redeem me and have mercy on me'—the washing of the hands.

11—'whose memory we celebrate on earth', invocation of the saints before the Secret Prayer and the Preface.

12—'Lift up your hearts' is in the Preface.

13—'And they sleep in peace'—the prayer for the dead.

14 & 15—'Forgive us our debts' and 'deliver us from evil' —from the Our Father.

16—'Deliver us, we pray Thee, O Lord'—said immediately after the Our Father.

p. 100 *To Night*: Glamaig—a mountain peak, 'a very ferocious one' in Skye, visible from Applecross; Eaglais Choluim (Church of Columba)—there are several, here on Staffa; Shieldaig— loch and glen. Wester Ross and Cromarty; Sunart—Ardnamurchan, Argyll—district and loch; Blaven/Blabhein—peak in Skye at head of Loch Scavaig; Morvern; Canisp—SW Sutherland on south side of Loch Assynt; Suilven—peak, southwest border of Sutherland; Quinag—mountain, Sutherland, north side of Loch Assynt; Colum Cille—Saint Columba; Uchd Eilein—'the place on the island' taken by earlier scholarship to be a proper name, the last resting-place of St Columba; Canach—the bog-cotton. Its white tufts on a long stem suggest tapers, and on Canna Island by Sanday Island there is a white flashing light as a beacon. This poem was written in 1950 but the text went missing. In 1970 Olive recovered it from memory, all but stanza 7, which she wrote anew. (The earlier text is on record.)

p. 102 *A Gossip Silenced*: This and the following two poems, along with 'The Glen of the Clearance' and 'V.E. Day 1945' were entered for the national contest for poetry in Scots organised by the Scottish Committee of the Arts Council of Great Britain to mark the Festival of Britain, 1951. The prizewinning poems of Olive Fraser, Alexander Scott and Sydney Goodsir Smith (equal first for lyrics) were, with other poems submitted, printed in 1952 as *New Scots Poetry*. Gloss: keep/ dwell in; machair/ low-lying meadow by riverside or sea-shore; steikin'/ (stitching), fixing or fashioning by piercing; maukin/ hare; tap/ top; bings/ heaps; merle/ blackbird; simmer/ summer.

p. 103 *All Sawles' Eve*: Gloss: yett/ gate; by my lane; alone; lauchin'/ laughing; winnock/ little window; lown/ serene; leal/ loyal; nieve/ the closed hand, but without the hostility of 'fist'; toom/ empty.

p. 104 *The Charity Child*: doucely/ gently, sweetly; couthily/ in a comforting manner; shoon/ shoes; bield/ shelter; saikless/ innocent; wrocht/ worked, toiled.

p. 105 *The Ballad of Dhruimbogle*: An excerpt only is given here. This ballad survives in manuscript, but lacking title and stanzas 1–7, and the text is incomplete, the ending only summarised in a prose note. There is a 'signature'—'Rory More MacLeod' a pseudonym for the contest perhaps. Olive apparently could not complete it in time for her intended entry in Section II of the 1951 contest, for a narrative poem in Scots. In Section III, for a play in Scots, she was awarded the third prize—for a nativity play for Christmas Eve called 'The Road to Glenlivet'. (There is a typescript in the National Library of Scotland.) Gloss: 8—rown/roan; lunt/glint; 9—doocit/dove-ecote; scraik, outshraik, skirl/ screeched, cried out discordantly; 10—yammering/ crying; clamjampherie/ rabble, gallimaufry; 11—hyowkit/ hauled away from; stour/ rising dust; 12—sclaiter/ scraping; bauchle/ clumsy, worn footwear; 13—cranreuch/ hoarfrost; 14—gowd marys/ marigolds; mools/ mould; 15—ramp/ move boisterously; trattled uncoly/ chattered greatly; 16—Od's yett/ God's gate—harmless exclamation; 17—sules/ seals; 18—bield/ cover, shelter; maud/ plaid; 21—hertes-heighth/ courage; dree/ suffering; speir/ beg for; 22—creeplin'/ creeping, rippling; soom/ swim; sweir/ unwilling, i.e. rough, line 4: O let the little stars shine out—; 24—blee/ hue; 25—swevens/ dreams, louted/bowed; 26—gaured whisht/ made be silent.

p.108 *Lazarus*: Gloss: weet/ wet; tint/ lost; kisted/ chested, coffined, ainly/ only.

p.108 *Lat my Demon be*: Leave my Daimon (genius) alone. Gloss: chaumer/ chamber; wauks/ is awake, alert, watches; yird/ earth, garden; loe/ love; carp/ speak (persistently).

p.111 *The Poet's Hours*: *angelus domini*/ 'And the angel of the Lord . . .': the opening of 'The Magnificat' gives its name to 'The Angelus' of evening prayer.

p.114 *The Little Waterhen*: The Latin phrases, in order from the 'Gloria' of the Mass: We praise Thee; We bless Thee; We adore Thee; We glorify Thee; We give Thee thanks, because of Thy great glory.)

p.116 *An Ancient Cathedral*: Probably St Machars, Old Aberdeen, a subject of tribute in other poems.

p.120 *Thought of the Bad Hat*: st.3, line 6 'And mothers lie' is incomplete.

HOSPITAL IN LONDON AND RECOVERING IN THE
NORTH 1956–1966

p.127 *Let there be no more angels . . .*: Britain has two white wild orchids, the greater butterfly orchid, *platanthera chlorantha,* called locally 'night violet' and 'white angel'—and *spiranthus chlorantha*, 'Lady's tresses' or 'sweet cullions' (testicles). The plant is venereal. The satyrion (here mis-spelled 'satyricon'!) is linked with the life-force of the satyrs; orchid derives its name from the Greek word for testicles because of its two-fold tuberous root. Persephone is queen of the underworld. This poem looks back to lyrics of 1936, 'Nocturnal to Poetry' and 'Envoi to Poetry'.

p.127 *Envoi*: After her first spell of illness in Bexley Hospital Olive went home in 1956, if only for a little while.

p.129 *The Poet to the Holy Ghost*: Tophet, biblical 'place of burning' to the south of Jerusalem in the valley of Hinnom, where carcases and filth from the city were burned; Yggdrasil—in Nordic mythology 'the world tree'; *dies Irae*—day of wrath/ the medieval poem by Thomas of Celano (c.1220) later incorporated into the Requiem for the Dead; *veni creator spiritus*/ Come, thou creator spirit: (Hymn by Fortunatus for Pentecost).

p.130 *Tigers*: this and another light poem 'Woodpecker Wood' not printed here are marked '. . . the poems I wrote when I had to take the chlorpromazine (sic) and felt as if I had been hammered down in a box and dropped below the Bermuda deep'. Chlorpromyzine was a new drug in 1956; Olive perhaps had never seen the word written.

p.135   *The Solace . . .*: Lena Stuart, Helena M. Stuart, who had been a fellow student at King's College, Aberdeen and renewed that friendship in the 1960s. See the Introduction, p.27.


THE 'WONDERFUL YEARS', ABERDEEN:
HOSPITAL AND HOLIDAYS 1970–1973

p.139   *Prayer to a Tree*: See Introduction, p.42.

p.139   *To A.M.J.*: again a title for Ann Maria Jeans, the beloved great-aunt.

p.140   *The Artist*: Antares—the farthest star, a very bright one. The poem contains an anagram on Oliver.

p.143   *To Dinah and Ronnie Garden*: Davidina Bonner *alias* Dinah, a close friend from College days onward, married Ronald Garden, also a fellow student. They were the first to welcome Olive back to Aberdeen in 1962.

p.145   *The Unwanted Child*: Betelgueuse (always spelled by the poet in this way, probably to avoid the danger in pronouncing the word with a soft 'g') is the largest star—bringer of all talents and honours. Algol, the dragon's eye in Perseus, the most unlucky star in the heavens, mischief-maker—'the winking star' because of the interrupted rhythm of its beams.

p.146   *To London*: Ben Dearg and Sgurr nan Gillean—mountain peaks in Skye, Algol the most malevolent star; Pegasus, horse of honour and friend of the muses; the Pleiades—the close cluster of stars in the constellation Taurus, in mythology seven daughters of Atlas—and so a brilliant cluster of friends—of poets in the French Renaissance.

p.148   *To Roman Stamm*: Roman Stamm—a war-wounded Polish marine, then working as gardener at Blair's College. He and his wife Betty were firm friends of Olive, who stood godmother to their baby daughter.

p.150   *The Corner Shop*: William McDougall, who married Olive's aunt Elizabeth Fraser, had a grocer's shop on the corner of Gilcomston Steps in Aberdeen. Olive's father, invalided by arthritis, lived with them in Elmfield Avenue and sometimes on better days came with them to the shop. See 'Requiem for Dives', p.90 and note.

p.151 *On Remembering an Attic Room in London*: the attic room was a bedsitting room in Bloomsbury, c/o Mrs Driscoll, 7 Regent Square, London WC2. Douglas Gibson, a poet and contemporary, had an attic room opposite and recalls Olive with pleasure and laughter. This during university vacations was a gathering place in town for Olive's Cambridge friends.

p.153 *To Christa Ahrens*: a young nurse from Germany working in Cornhill Hospital. The 'iron mountain' from fairy tale; lustres/ gleams, also periods of 5 years.

p.157 *The Adder of Quinag*: Meg Myles in the far north of Scotland surprised a young adder which did not flinch as it had never encountered man. She told Olive the story. The adder of Quinag comes also in the stanza Olive rewrote in 1970 for 'To Night'. This poem is in demand for anthologies and the creature on its way into folklore. 'Quinag of the adder?'

p.163 *If I forget thee*: Father Alexander Burgess died in 1975. He was very frail in his last years. A Franciscan Friar, O.S.F. Min. Cap., he was from 1950 onwards a mainstay to Olive Fraser. After service in different regions he became Guardian at Erith, but ended his days near Uddingston, Glasgow. He kept in touch through letter and visit throughout—see the Introduction.

p.164 *Remembering a Child's Christmas Eve*: an early version is entitled 'Remembering a Child's Christmas Eve beyond the Howford Bridge'; century - word play is intended on 'centaury' the plant. See 'To a Dog' and note.

p.165 *The Dipper's Nest that overhangs the River* has 'River Nairn' in one version of the title.
*To Alice*: Alice was the wife of John MacDonald, first cousin to Olive's mother and son of the Mrs Isabella MacDonald in whose house Olive was born.

p.177 *Voyage of a Ship: a Childhood Memory*: the 'Medic' made the war-time journey to Melbourne in 1914/15. Probably her household 'providing' was shipped out aboard it to Mrs Fraser in Australia. The Cawdor Hills are within sight of 'Redburn' in Nairn.

p.182 *The River*: There is a blank in line 8: there is a word missing in the original manuscript.

p.182 *An Old Purse*: again a tribute to Miss Jeans: a stony crown—King's College, Old Aberdeen; the cobbled street—Nairn; the scarlet gown—the *toga rubra,* red toga, academic gown of the student of a Scottish university, worn to classes in those days.

p.183 *To a Dog*: centaury is *fel terrae,* earth gall, 'the bitterest herb known'—the pink centaury *centaurium minus,* that grows in Scotland. Olive pronounced it 'century'. It comes into 'Remembering a Child's Christmas Eve'.

p.183 *A Shelf of Books*: See Introduction, p.43 and 'Desperate for Love'.

p.184 *On the Virtue of a Single Meeting*: fief/ a debt or obligation, especially of a military nature.

p.185 *Desperate for Love*: The fair virgin: Virgo, zodiac sign for August 'figures' the Blessed Virgin, whose great feast falls in that month, and is a correspondence used in renaissance poetry and drawn on by Olive Fraser. Compare 'A Shelf of Books', p.183 and note.

LAST YEARS 1974–1976

p.191 *I have such joy*: Cygnus—the constellation Cygnus the swan is in the form of a cross.

p.192 *What is this need*: There is a blank space in line 4 in the copies available.

p.193 *To My Mother*: line 2—evil (to) o; anagrammatic presence of Olive.

p.195 *Dreamed 2nd January 1975: Midnight low mass in a Jesuit Church*: 2nd January is the Feast of the Blessed Name of Jesus. Both place and date focus on the name of Jesus. The name of the poet, in anagram, is here between 'My Life' and 'Thee'. 'Zou mow sas agape' translates as 'My Life I love thee'. Olive, who did not know Greek, probably had in her memory the Greek phrase transliterated as used by Byron in 'Maid of Athens' and recalls it imperfectly.

p.199 *Sanctuary/The Kootenay ram*: the Kootenay ram is a threatened species of the Canadian Rockies. Olive is remembering 'Krag, the Kootenay Ram', a famous short story by Ernest Thompson Seton, popular writer for children in the 1920s. See Introduction p.31.

p.202 *On Meeting Twentysix Swans in a River*: recalling the holiday spent canoeing on the River Wye with Oliver Zangwill in the summer when Olive was 26 years old.